D0949916

WAIT, BLINK

WAIT, BLINK

A PERFECT PICTURE
OF INNER LIFE

GUNNHILD ØYEHAUG

TRANSLATED FROM THE NORWEGIAN
BY KARI DICKSON

FARRAR, STRAUS AND GIROUX
NEW YORK

Farrar, Straus and Giroux
175 Varick Street, New York 10014

Printed in the United States of America
Originally published in Norwegian in 2008 by Kolon forlag,
Norway, as *Vente, blinke: eit perfekt bilete av eit personleg indre*
English translation published in the United States
by Farrar, Straus and Giroux
First American edition, 2018

Library of Congress Cataloging-in-Publication Data
Names: Øyehaug, Gunnhild, 1975– author. | Dickson, Kari, translator.
Title: Wait, blink : a perfect picture of inner life / Gunnhild Øyehaug ;
translated from the Norwegian by Kari Dickson.
Other titles: Vente, blinke. English
Description: First American edition. | New York : Farrar, Straus and
Giroux [2018] | "Originally published in Norwegian in 2008 by
Kolon forlag, Norway, as Vente, blinke"—T.p. Verso
Identifiers: LCCN 2017047944 | ISBN 9780374285890 (hardcover)
Classification: LCC PT8952.25.Y44 V4613 2018 | DDC 839.823/8—dc23
LC record available at https://lccn.loc.gov/2017047944

Designed by Jonathan D. Lippincott

Our books may be purchased in bulk for promotional, educational,
or business use. Please contact your local bookseller or the Macmillan
Corporate and Premium Sales Department at 1-800-221-7945, extension
5442, or by e-mail at MacmillanSpecialMarkets@macmillan.com.

www.fsgbooks.com
www.twitter.com/fsgbooks • www.facebook.com/fsgbooks

1   3   5   7   9   10   8   6   4   2

I am the world.
But the world is not me.
      —Daniil Kharms

I

MORNINGS

1

Here we see Sigrid. It's nine o'clock in the morning, it's January, and the 2008 January light fills the room sharply, yet reliably, with a color temperature of 5600 kelvins, which is the normal color temperature for daylight, and consequently is the color temperature of the bulbs in the large spotlights you have to set up outside the window if you're going to simulate daylight in a room in a movie, and then turn on so they'll *shine* through the glass with a light that to those of us passing by outside, and who only see the spotlights and not the effect in the room, seems far too bright to simulate daylight. Well: Sigrid is sitting in this natural daylight, at a desk by the wall. The expression on her face is thoughtful, and her face is framed by hair, hair that she sometimes pulls, without realizing she's doing it, possibly, as Sigrid's face reveals that she is utterly absorbed by what she's holding up in front of her, what she's looking at: a miniature portrait of a man, in black and white, on a book jacket. When she's engrossed like this, her face goes slack. It's as if her eyes are what are holding up her face, wide-open and alert. And in the center of Sigrid's eyes are her pupils; we are *drawn in* toward Sigrid's pupils, which are black as ink and closed to us—like two periods!—even though we would have liked to imagine that we could stare our way in through her pupils, as if through a narrow black funnel, stare our way into her head and become absorbed, and become the thoughts in her head, like the water in the water, the air in the air, the flesh on the hand holding this piece of paper, or the wood in the tree outside her window that's standing there shivering in the January air, and doesn't know that she knows it exists!

•

Sigrid is twenty-three and studying literature at the University of Bergen. She's the kind of literature student who has photographs of literary theorists on her wall, photocopied from textbooks and stuck up with Blu Tack, which shows through at the top of the sheet of copy paper. She's also the kind of literature student who has a print of Van Gogh's sunflowers on the wall because they *mean* something to her (there's something about the yellowness, the grotesqueness, the newly opened and the withered, "life" and "death," the hopelessness with which the sunflowers twist out of the vase and stand there hanging their absurd one-eyed faces). (There's something about the way they're so *alone*, and yet so grotesquely open.) And she has so much she'd like to tell to someone who's willing to listen, naturally. She normally talks to Magnus about things like this, things she's seen, things she's read, things she's thought, things she's analyzed, pondered, and thought about and thought about as she brushed her teeth, went to bed, showered, and had breakfast the next morning, things that have expanded to be more than things, things that have grown inside her like a huge sunflower that now fills her entire being and stares at her from inside her head with its big one-eyed face, until she's ready to burst and phones Magnus to tell him about it. But Magnus has moved to Oslo and gotten himself a girlfriend, and even though she's sure that at one point or another they *will* split up, because after all, it's obvious that she and Magnus are the perfect couple, she has a strong feeling that she's lost again. Once again the world has put up its hand and said: *you!* you can get straight back into your own head.

•

When Sigrid was a child, she often became attached to things in nature for want of any feeling of contact with people. She became attached to the mountains behind the house and the stars, in particular, the stars over the mountains at night. She would sit on her bed, which was right by the window, with her chin on the windowsill, and look up at the mountains, which were often completely white, as it was usually winter when she sat like this and looked at the mountains that were almost bright white, and the Big Dipper that hung shining above the mountains, and moved slowly along the ridge. And she looked at all the other stars, how they sparkled and shone, as though they were alive. And Sigrid looked up at them and thought: you understand me. If no one else understands me, you're always there! Sometimes it brought tears to her eyes because she felt the connection between herself and the stars so intensely. They *were* her, and the white mountains were her, and the black sky.

•

Luckily, every now and then, Jon English would lift her chin with his finger, and her head, which had been bent deep in thought, and her long dark hair (she imagined) were lifted slowly and full of promise by Jon English's finger under her chin and she looked straight into a pair of eyes that were so clear and blue and full of love and understanding. His eyes shone in just the same way they did in *Against the Wind*. And Sigrid shone back. And one day, she thought, as she sat there with her chin on the windowsill, looking at the stars, this would actually happen in real life as well, she would be sitting with her head bent deep in thought like now, and someone would lift her chin with his finger.

•

In other words: Sigrid also shines brightly, her inner life is luminous, only not many people have seen it, her secret, sparkling light. Definitely not Magnus, that's for sure. And she's completely forgotten Jon English. But right now, as she sits here holding the book with the photograph of the author, she gets the strange feeling that perhaps it doesn't matter, the whole thing with Magnus. The other day she went into a bookshop, as she normally does when she's got nowhere to go and doesn't dare go to a café on her own because she can't face giving herself a pep talk before she goes in and then having to encourage herself every second that she sits there, because it's quite obvious that she's not there with anyone; she went into a bookshop instead. It was one of those days when she felt like the white mountains and the stars and the dark, dark night. Which no one, *no one* saw. She wandered between the shelves, took down one book after another, and then randomly she pulled out a book that had the fantastic and hopeful life-affirming title *An Empty Chair*. The very thing she was looking for. Somewhere to sit, in life. Someone who wanted her to sit there with them. When she turned the book over to read the back, she met the eyes of the author, Kåre Tryvle. Yes, that was exactly what happened, she felt that he *met* her eyes, Kåre Tryvle. She stood there looking at his face. She thought he was very handsome, of course, he was dark and there was something Jon English–ish about his square features, a more distinguished Jon English, but it was the eyes that kept her transfixed. It was as if they saw deep inside her, as though all the time she had been wandering around feeling so infinitely lonely, these eyes, which *saw* it, which saw her infinite loneliness, had been there in the bookshelf. Eyes that seemed to say: hello, you. It could well be that she felt like this because of the illusion that's created when the subject of a picture looks straight at the observer (painter or photographer): no matter where you place yourself in relation to the picture, you seem to have eye contact. And it might well be the tiniest bit nuts to feel like that, that he *saw* her, but Sigrid didn't reflect on it at all, she just felt a sublime and stomach-lurching *oh*, and took a step back as a result, which meant that she reversed into a stroller that was coming toward her and she had to say: sorry! to the mother pushing it, and the mother said: no worries, there's not much room here. And then, because Sigrid had fallen into a kind of trance, which meant that she'd forgotten that she was still part of the world's everyday movements, like stepping aside if someone wants to get by with a stroller, the mother with the stroller had to say: do you mind moving a bit, so I can get to the end of the alphabet, which made Sigrid blush, and look at the book she was holding, and say: yes, of course, I'm only at *T*, so sorry, and then she had to move out of the way so the stroller-pushing mother could get past to the end of the alphabet, and she turned away to hide her redness, a blush that wasn't only caused by this end-of-alphabet situation, because wasn't that just incredible? Symbolic, in a way, that she had been standing here with the book in her hand, with the eyes that had somehow been there waiting? Surely it was destiny? That on a mountain and star day like today, a *stroller* came and bumped into her at just that moment?

•

And when she got home later and read his poems, she felt that his poems were just like his eyes. That they saw right in. The poems were clear: "Sit here," she read, right after the book had quoted César Vallejo: "Beloved the people who sit down." Her eyes welled up. *Beloved the people who sit down.* She could look at the portrait and stroke the book and think: we understand each other. But you don't know that. You, Kåre, she thought, even though she noticed that when she thought his name, it somehow didn't feel quite natural. She tried to say it out loud now and then, *Kåre*, but her voice sounded distorted whenever she said it, it wasn't a natural name to say. She'd even looked it up in a name book, to see what it meant, and it didn't mean, as she'd hoped, "the seer" or "protection" or "home," or anything profound like that, any symbolic indication that he *was* in fact the one she had been searching for. Kåre just meant "the one with the curly hair." But it didn't matter, after all, it didn't change the deep mystic bond that she felt between herself and his eyes on the back cover of the book. It was as though she knew who he was, as though it was real.

2

Yes, who are you, Tryvle? Here we see Kåre Tryvle. Not in miniature, but full-sized. And where is he? In Bergen. In Bergen, Sigrid's town. In the same town where a girl of twenty-three is sitting in a room where the sharp January light comes in through the roof window, looking at a miniature portrait of Kåre Tryvle with the feeling that he represents hope in life, that very same man is standing, at nine o'clock in the morning, in front of an audience of about two hundred men and maybe thirty women, all dressed in suits, at the Hotel Norge. They're at a business conference in Bergen, and Kåre has been asked to provide the morning's entertainment. Kåre stands in front of his audience, dressed in dark, worn jeans and a hoodie, with a pair of new blue Adidas sneakers on his feet, and we can tell from his mouth that he's talking, and it's almost possible to see from the lines around his mouth that he's saying something funny—*et violà*: the audience laughs. He holds up a book and says: it's true, you can read it for yourselves, here. You *have* the perfect golf swing in you, you just need to find it. The audience laughs again. So there you have it, *Golf Can't Be This Simple*, Kåre says. But, he continues, life is not always as simple as golf, unfortunately. And then he picks up a novel "that I have written myself," as he says, and starts to read.

•

So, who are you, Kåre? If we look at him, knowing that he's forty-three, and see that he's wearing jeans and a hoodie and new Adidas sneakers, we might think that he's trying desperately to seem younger than he actually is. Or we might think that he doesn't care that he seems to be trying desperately to look younger than he is; he *likes* wearing hoodies. He doesn't give a damn that this might make it look as though he's having a midlife crisis. Hoodies reflect who he is and always has been. He doesn't wear a shirt and suit. It would never cross his mind. If that means he has to go to a funeral in jeans and a hoodie, then so be it. It should be noted that the new Adidas sneakers are not quite in keeping with Kåre's image; he prefers for everything to look used and worn. His hoodie is a little frayed, his jeans as well, dark and kind of rock 'n' roll. He's flung his big black down jacket on a chair behind him, the kind of down jacket with a fur-lined hood (only he's taken the fur trim off, so it looks more like an anorak), and some headphones with a skull logo are sticking out of its pocket. They are quality headphones; Kåre wants only the best when he's walking through town listening to music. They have to look cool too, which Skullcandy headphones most definitely do. If we were to turn on the iPod in his pocket, we'd hear what music he was listening to on his way to the Hotel Norge and discover that he'd had to stop PJ

Harvey's beautiful song "This Is Love" just as she sings: "I wanna chase you round the table, I wanna touch your head," one of Kåre's ten all-time favorite lines from pop songs, because of its simplicity and directness. That is to say, he's shouted *I wanna touch your head!* many a time over a table in a bar late at night, even when he wasn't coming on to anyone—though, to be completely honest, he's shouted it when he *was* coming on to someone too, and it actually had a positive effect (after he's touched the person he's shouted at on the head)—but the *main point* for Kåre is the quality of the sentence, the simple straightforwardness of saying, I wanna touch your head. Kåre believes that every sentence should be like that, be it pop or literature, and that is the primary reason he shouts *I wanna touch your head!* over pub tables.

·

The truth is, if he weren't so hopeless at singing, Kåre would have preferred to be a musician. He's musical and knows intuitively that he would be a fucking fantastic front man in a band. He just can't sing. That is to say, he can sing, but when he made his debut as the vocalist for his band, Jimmy and the Aunts, at the age of seventeen, he quickly discovered that his voice, about which he had been supremely confident in his bedroom and the bathroom, did indeed have its limitations, which had come as a bit of a shock to him. The fact was that he *wasn't* the world's best singer and rock star, the fact was that his voice actually couldn't reach the high notes, that he had problems getting back in tune if he drifted, and so had sung a whole song off-key, to an audience of mute-faced youth clubbers.

·

The besuited Hotel Norge audience, on the other hand, is laughing. Kåre's protagonist has just fallen on the stairs at IKEA in front of a couple of teenage girls. As he reads and looks out over his audience, Kåre is suddenly filled with a kind of disgust at the situation. It's inauthentic, he thinks as he reads (it's often astonished him that he's able to think and observe as much as he does while he's reading and apparently engaging in something else, what he's reading, for example), this is inauthentic, he's standing in front of an audience of suits, making them laugh, they're laughing at his protagonist, just as he hoped they would, and suddenly he feels out of touch with the situation. Is that because his own life is such a mess, is that why he feels like this? Has the state of his life caught up with him as he stands here in front of an audience? The state of his life, which he thought he could escape by coming here to Bergen, but which is now running down his spine with the chill of bog water?

•

The state of his life: The fact that it's been over with Wanda, his girlfriend of three years, for a week now. That he hasn't tried to contact her, and she hasn't tried to contact him. That there's been total and utter silence. That he doesn't know whether he misses her or not, and in that sense, it really *is* over. That he's become cynical and cold again.

•

Yes, that is the state of his life, the real state of things, for Kåre Tryvle, this very moment as he stands in front of an audience in the Hotel Norge.

3

For Sigrid, on the other hand, in her room where the light from the skylight falls straight onto the miniature portrait of Kåre Tryvle on the back of her book, things are closing in. She looks around and catches her own eye in the mirror that's hanging on the wall above her desk. Here she sits, in her room, a book in her hands. Here she sits: on the wall in front of her is a picture of Paul de Man, a Belgian literary theorist, and on the wall beside her is a mirror in which she can see herself, and on the sloping wall behind her she's hung up a print of Van Gogh's sunflowers, which *means* something to her, and in her hands she has a book. Is there anyone else in the room? No. This is Sigrid, in her room. This is Sigrid, in her head. As always! The situation is so typical of her life. What a typical situation—that she should try to understand and understand and that everything should have meaning and more meaning, but the only understanding *she* could get was from a pair of eyes on the back of a book, or the stars over the mountains at night—it strikes her as she sits there with the book in front of her, and the walls suddenly feel like walls and the ceiling feels like a ceiling, as sometimes happens when the magic of the moment that you feel there is hope disappears and all that remains is this: walls, and ceilings, and walls. And ceilings.

•

And oversized men's shirts. Sigrid looks at the cursor flashing on the computer screen in front of her. That's what she should be doing right now, writing about those oversized men's shirts, not wasting time trying to understand the look in Kåre Tryvle's eyes. She needs to find the scene in *Lost in Translation* where the main character, Charlotte, wanders around in a brightly lit hotel room in Tokyo wearing an oversized man's shirt, and is the very incarnation of a vulnerable woman. Yes.

•

Sigrid's phone beeps. It's a message from Magnus! that says: "Idea about girls in oversized men's shirts OK. Send draft Friday." That means he's back from Prague then, she thinks, and writes: "Back from Prague? Good trip?" Oh, Prague! He'd called her to tell her that he'd bought surprise tickets for Elida, his girlfriend, who was writing her thesis about Kafka's *The Castle*, and Sigrid had mused on the fact that he'd called *her* as soon as he'd bought them, so maybe he was actually thinking about Sigrid, that is to say, *subconsciously* thinking about Sigrid when he bought the tickets, and not Elida. Oh, why can't you see that, she thought, and meanwhile pretended to be really pleased for him.

•

But she gets no answer from Magnus, she isn't told, right away, that they had a lovely trip to Prague. What does that mean, the fact that he doesn't answer right away? That they had a bad time? Or the opposite, that they had such a great trip that he forgot Sigrid as soon as he said what he needed to? She looks at Kåre, whom she's put down on top of a pile of other books on her desk. He's much older than her; it says on the back flap that he was born in 1965. That means he's . . .'75, '85, '95, 2005 = 40, plus 2008 − 2005 = 3, which makes a total of 40 + 3 = 43. Exactly twenty years older than her! She lifts him up to look into his eyes again, but she doesn't get the same magical feeling of a mysterious bond between them, and has to put him down and instead click her way on the computer screen to a document titled: "The Windswept Woman." The title is inspired by a poem by Geir Gulliksen, in which a woman wanders around in a crumpled man's shirt with bare legs and feet, and the bed behind her looks like a windswept breakwater. Sigrid loves the poem, but recently she's started to notice that whenever women are supposed to come across as fragile and vulnerable in films or literature, they're always wearing oversized men's shirts, with bare legs. And they often also have tousled hair. She's begun to write an essay about it, and has now been given the green light to send it in to the literary periodical published by students at the University of Oslo. The fact is, she can't bear it, as she told Magnus: I can't bear any more women in over-sized men's shirts. What is it about the shirts that makes them so incredibly cute and irresistible? Take, for example, that Norwegian film I can't remember the name of, Sigrid started, where Maria Bonnevie plays a woman who's two things: provocative and sexy with red lips and a tight red dress, and lost and vulnerable with tousled hair and no makeup in an oversized man's shirt. It's true! Next piece of evidence: the lovely film *Mr. & Mrs. Smith*, with Brangelina Pitt. Angelina is two things: sexy in suspenders, armed to the hilt with guns, until it turns out she's actually a gentle, loving woman—in an oversized man's shirt with bare legs. Third piece of evidence: in the film *A History of Violence*, there's the wife of the former gangster whose past catches up with him, and *after* they've had super-charged and steamy make-up sex on a staircase, where she's banged into the steps and clearly thinks it's the peak of physical delight, she appears in an oversized man's shirt, and thus—having first been extremely sexy and extremely grown-up, she then looks like a little girl. Fourth piece of evidence, Sigrid argued, holding up four fingers to show how far she'd gotten, and had to hold down her little finger as it wanted to join the others: four is the young princess in *Enchanted*. After she's fallen through a portal from the cartoon world, where everything is pink and rosy, and she's about to marry her prince—which is to say, after she's fallen into the real world, she starts to experience more complex feelings after meeting the hard-nosed lawyer, and all of a sudden she's sitting there on the hard-nosed lawyer's sofa late one evening, all vulnerable. And is wearing a far too big, badly buttoned pair of male pajamas. And is utterly adorable. Magnus laughed. "Pair of male pajamas," can you actually say that? Magnus asked. Fifth piece of evidence: the main character in *Lost in Translation* also wears an oversized man's shirt when she's alone in her hotel room. Which struck Sigrid as a bit odd, really, given that the film was directed by a woman. Anyway, then there's the poem by Geir Gulliksen, Sigrid said, which I love. The only problem is that the woman whom the poem's *I* obviously loves, or has loved, is wearing a crumpled man's shirt and is padding around with bare legs and bare feet! But describing the bed as a windswept breakwater *is* fantastic, Magnus said. Yes, Sigrid agreed. It is. It *is* fantastic. She sat for a while and imagined the windswept breakwater, a white breakwater that went straight out into the sea, and it was dark and cold around the white bed that ended in the cold, black water, and the wind was blowing every which way. It's enough to make you shiver, Sigrid said. Suddenly she felt that she had a breakwater just like that inside her. A small, white breakwater in the midst of all the great, heavy darkness. But what, she said, going back to her original point, is so fucking (oh, a word she seldom used) lovely about windswept small women in big shirts? Eh? I don't know, Magnus said, but it *is* cute, we like it! Yes, but why? Sigrid asked. Have you men analyzed it yourselves? Magnus laughed and said: no. You'll have to do that for us. I fucking well will, Sigrid said. On the other hand, isn't it comfortable for you to wear oversized shirts? Magnus asked, and she hit him over the head with a collection of Geir Gulliksen's poetry. Which is precisely what she should be doing right now; well, that is to say, not hitting someone over the head with Geir Gulliksen's poetry, but analyzing the phenomenon, women in oversized shirts, as an expression of a certain aesthetic *understanding*.

•

Before she starts, she catches a glimpse of herself in the mirror that hangs on the wall beside her desk and she sees that she's not strikingly beautiful, but has messy brown hair, big lips and thick eyebrows, and a scrunched-up look on her face.

And she's wearing a homemade sweater that her aunt knitted for her uncle, but got wrong, in a kind of bobbly light brown wool that makes her look like a teddy bear. An oversized light brown woolly sweater clearly does not have the same effect as an oversized man's shirt; she doesn't look sweet and vulnerable. She looks stupid and fat. Perhaps the lack of sweetness and vulnerability has something to do with the fact that she hasn't got bare legs. She's actually wearing a pair of burgundy sweatpants in a kind of shiny velvet, which are tucked into a pair of thick socks, which in turn have been stuffed into a pair of woolly slippers. She looks absolutely *terrible*!

4

Here, on the other hand, we see the film director Linnea (twenty-seven) standing in an oversized light blue man's shirt and with only a pair of briefs on underneath, at nine o'clock in the morning, on the eleventh floor of a hotel in Copenhagen. She stands by the window, looking out, and is really rather beautiful, if we say so ourselves. She's thinking how empty the city is now, utterly empty. The light blue shirt that she's wearing belongs to Göran Fältberg (forty-seven), professor of comparative literature at Uppsala University. We would have loved to point at Linnea and say to Sigrid: "Here is someone you can interview about oversized men's shirts," but sadly, that's impossible. So, is this young film director aware that her current attire means she has joined the ranks of young, vulnerable women in oversized men's shirts? No, Linnea doesn't give it a thought. But is she vulnerable? Yes. The morning sun shines faintly through a layer of mist, and she can see long gray airplane bodies pushing through the clouds like weightless nails. But it all might as well be nothing.

Because: Göran isn't here. The whole city might as well not be here, but she can feel the pane of glass that separates her from the city down there, she can feel it against her cheek, and she is there, she is there in a very particular and *palpable* way, with her fingertips against the glass. Because Göran Fältberg isn't there and she's longing for him. Linnea presses her nose against the window. There's a knock at the door. Linnea jumps, we can see two clear stripes on the glass where her nostrils have breathed warm air. The rest of the window-pane where she's been standing is still steamed up. She goes over to the door and opens it, and finds Robert, her producer, standing outside.

•

Robert lowers his eyes when he sees how little she's wearing. He wasn't prepared for it, he'd expected her to be dressed and ready to go. But there she is, in only a shirt, the skin on her chest and legs exposed. He's never seen her skin before, other than on her face, neck, and hands. He starts to perspire and mumbles something that Linnea doesn't hear. Hmm? she says, and can't help smiling, there is something about Robert, something mumbly. His clothes are always elegant and ex-pensive, but they somehow manage to look ill-fitting, they crease or twist and sit a bit tight over the shoulder, it's al-most as if Robert's clothes have barely consented to be on his body. As if they had screamed: okay, fine, we'll do it, having first slammed a few doors. Robert looks up at her, his eyes wide open, as though he's told himself that he *has to* pull himself together and look at her: I must have gotten the time wrong, Robert says. What time is it? Linnea asks. Nine o'clock, Robert tells her. Oh, Linnea says, sorry. I wasn't paying attention. I'll be as quick as I can. Can we meet in reception in half an hour? That's fine, Robert mumbles to his shoes. I'll just go back to . . . (he has to look at her again, slide his eyes up her body from her bare feet, up the shirt, to her chest, neck, face—he blushes) . . . to my room. Okay; Linnea smiles, as she can see he's trying not to look, and closes the door.

•

While Linnea jumps into the shower, showers, gets out of the shower, and starts to take some clothes out of the suitcase that she's left on a small sofa, we might ask, who is Linnea? If we think of the woodland flower she's named after (a small pink and white bell-like flower that grows on the forest floor, which looks as though it's blushing bashfully because you're standing there above it with your hiking boots planted stoutly in the heather as you bend down to get a closer look at it), we might expect her to be a small, delicate person. Which is, indeed, the case. Linnea is small and slight and often walks with her head down, as though she were a small bell-like flower who wanted to keep things to herself, who blushed at the thought of anyone looking at her. Exquisite is what she is.

•

As a child, Linnea split her time between the antique shop that her parents ran and a home full of antique furniture. Before she started school, she spent part of the day at the antique shop and the other part with her parents in their living room, where they used to show films and slides on an old projector. Linnea loved it, she loved sitting in the dark, but was it actually the film she watched? No. Linnea loved to watch the beam of light from the projector and the swirling dust that seemed to be trapped inside it. That was where she wanted to be: there with the light beam and dancing dust, with the smell of the canvas and the knowledge that her parents were sitting close together on the rococo sofa behind her, engrossed in the film, barely visible, like two rococo ornaments, in the dark. Not interested in her, and not interested in the fact that she was sitting looking at the beam of light, not the film, and that for her it was incomprehensible, pure magic, that the pictures were carried on the dusty light beam only to appear on the canvas. They noticed none of this. When film showings were a thing of the past and the ages of VHS and then DVD had started, she forgot the beam of light for a while. Until she was seventeen and saw a chandelier in her parents' antique shop. The chandelier hung in a dark corner of the shop and gave off a glittering, self-contained play of light. Suddenly she remembered: the light from the projector, the dust dancing in the beam, sitting there looking at it. And she must have thought, *oh*. And she was compelled to ask if she could have the chandelier, only to hear the word "no." It was far too valuable. But what if it was what she wanted more than anything in the world? "No." But, she thought, she *was* the glittering yet contained play of light from the chandelier! And every time she saw a chandelier later, she thought about who she was: the closed play of light.

•

At film school, this was her greatest wish: to be able to film something that could *show* this play of light. And preferably show it on a semi-perforated screen, so that she could set up spotlights behind the screen, and shine them on the audience through the screen, so they would gasp in wonder. An "Oooohhh" would ripple through the room.

•

But: that's not possible, her lecturer told her. How do you think your audience will be able to see anything if you light the screen from behind? The screen would be white, the film faded to nothing. It's not possible. Oh, Linnea thought. She was too old now to ask the question: "But what if it's what I want more than anything in the world?"

•

In other words, Linnea hasn't had much luck with her wishes in life, and now she's standing by the window again, fresh out of the shower, in her underwear, holding a sweater in her hands and wishing that Göran were there. But is he? No.

•

(For your information: at this precise moment, while Linnea is standing by the window in Copenhagen, Göran Fältberg is lying asleep in his bed at home in Uppsala. Both he and his wife have overslept considerably this morning; his wife is lying beside him and the room is filled with their regular breathing. It's dark and cool, and the cover of the duvet that's wrapped around the husband and wife like two cocoons is white. Göran's chin has fallen to his chest, his eyes look sunken, his hair is short and white, as is his beard, and in the dark, the whiteness makes him look almost supernatural. He is dreaming, an uneasy dream, about some corridors at the university that just get longer and longer the farther he walks down them; unsettled by the fluorescent tube on the ceiling that's flickering, he holds out his keys and rattles them, which seems a very odd thing to do, Göran thinks in his dream, but he shakes and rattles them more and more intensely as he walks along the endless corridors, and it almost feels like he's been hypnotized by the flickering lights reflected in the flashing keys. So that is where Göran is, in his bed in Uppsala, in his dream of the rattling keys, at precisely the moment that Linnea stands by the window and wishes he were in Copenhagen.)

5

And here we see the artist Trine (thirty-two), who would rather have been called Tracey Emin (if she'd had the choice), but she isn't, sitting in an oversized dressing gown, looking out the window at the other windows that face onto the back courtyard of the cheap hotel where she's staying. It's nine o'clock in the morning of that same January day, and as far as she can tell, Oslo is functioning as it should; people are walking to work through the peculiar grayish white light of Slottsparken, between the black tree trunks and over the duck pond, covered with the thinnest crust of ice, and over the grass, which is probably thick with frost but is bare of snow. Trine, who is quite pleased that she's called Trine, which after all is a kind of Norwegian version of Tracey, which is the name of her greatest idol, Tracey Emin, rubs her cold feet against each other and then turns to watch some walruses on television. They swim purposefully through greenish-blue water.

•

If it had been seventeen months ago, she would have been sitting here with a cup of coffee and a cigarette. The coffee would be steaming hot, and her cigarette would glow whenever she took a drag with her sensual mouth. If it had been seventeen months ago, she would have drunk too much yesterday, or, to put it another way, she would have drunk as much as she always drank, too much, whereas in fact it wasn't too much, as it was exactly what she always drank. She would have sat here regretting she'd flashed her tits, not because she had shown them, but because she knew it would be interpreted as "aggressive performance," an artistic expression by a woman who wasn't afraid to use her whole disgusting self, but it *wasn't* about that at all, it was simply good old-fashioned flashing, in protest, in revenge. An idiotic revenge, really, because the man she wanted to avenge herself on (Knut, forty-four), wasn't even there, was conspicuous by his absence, in fact. In that sense it was a kind of cosmic, universal revenge, on everything and everyone, because her life was crap. *Go fuck yourselves.* It was that simple, that stupid. But it was awful, Trine would have thought, not to be able to do something as banal and stupid without it being interpreted as "aggressive performance." *Has she used herself in her art to such an extent that there is no longer any division between what she does in her private life and in her public life?* she'd have commented loudly to herself, pulling a face. Fuck that, Trine would have said to her cup of coffee, because in many ways it was a calculated risk that something of the sort might happen; only, if the truth be told, it was a *little* tiresome all the same. She couldn't exactly go around *explaining* everything she did, saying "this is art" or "that is not art" or "that can be seen as something in the gray area between art and not art," or "you'll have to ask me later if that was art," or "please see this as the individual Trine's personal opinion," but "this, on the other hand, the fact that I'm offending you, is in my role as an artist—Trine the individual would never do that." Fuck. "Fuck," Trine would have said out loud and laughed, as she thought that "fuck" was such a *ridiculous word, absurdly unradical, absurd in its total lack of content as a word, and yet, so effective.* She would have regretted kissing Urban, a short, fumbling curator from up north, simply to keep herself upright, simply as revenge. But then, what's the point of regret, she would have said, taking a sip of her coffee: What, she would have said, is, then taken a drag of her cigarette, the point? Fuck that. Fuck again! Fuck, you need to get out of my discourse, you lovely word, she would have said. You lovely little word.

•

But instead Trine had to put her head in her hands. There would have been too much noise in her head, a ringing in her ears, the music had been too loud yesterday. Seventeen months ago, head in hands, she would have pictured the face of Knut, the great curator from the east, whom she'd loved and lost. Whom she'd once seduced, about a year before that, by grabbing him between the legs outside a restroom in the art gallery and whom she'd had an extremely passionate on-and-off relationship with ever since. She would have, seventeen months ago, sat here and remembered Knut's face saying "I love you, you were right," at the train station early one morning and then, shoulders hunched in his leather jacket, he disappeared into the crowd, after she, night after night, had buried her face in his chest and said that she was sure that he loved her, without him saying anything in response, but now, now that she was about to take the train west, she somehow mystically knew that she would never see him again. Enough, she tells her hands, seventeen months ago, in exactly the same room in exactly the same hotel, I've seen Knut's face enough now, spoken enough nonsense, love doesn't exist, I've allowed myself to love someone, what a mistake, she says, and laughs at the last sentence. "I've allowed myself to love someone, what a mistake," what a clichéd sentence, what a cliché of an experience, what a cliché that he should say that, it sounded like a *script*, the end of a film, which he then followed up with an email that said, "This won't work. I'm a crater, and you are too. And crater plus crater doesn't work." What a cliché, what a cliché! that she'd hoped he would turn up all the same, at the opening yesterday, but he didn't. She needs to meet someone from the south, she tells herself, seventeen months ago, that's what she needs. Someone from the south. People are decent there, they're not short and fumbling like northerners, they're not big and brutal like easterners, and they haven't been destroyed by intense internal noise like us westerners. It's perfectly clear, she says to her hands, it has to be someone from the south. But: it wouldn't work anyway. It's all just more trouble. But she will, *yes*! She will! She'll make a quilt that says "I only want to be loved." But she can't, damn, Tracey Emin's already used quilting. Or was it a quilt? No, it wasn't! It was neon. "Just Love Me" written in pink neon. It was only yesterday that she saw it, at the exhibition, where she'd been part of the opening, with her performance "half naked, half dressed," out in the foyer, wearing a straitjacket on top and a G-string below. She'd found the words "Just Love Me" in a book about Tracey Emin that she'd sat looking at behind some bookshelves as she got steadily more drunk after the performance and should really have stood up, and in her drunken state she was blown away by the simple statement in pink neon, *just love me*, and started to cry, until Urban came and found her and she decided that kissing him might help the situation. Jesus! How quickly is it possible to forget something? It normally takes years before she forgets things and can use them in her art and think that she's being original, but this time it took less than a night. It must be (a) all the noise, (b) all the alcohol, (c) all the smoking, (d) all the stupid kissing with short curators from up north, just to help her stay on her feet, and forget Knut, from the east, (e) all the flashing, (f) sleeping on the steps outside the hotel, (g) being carried up the steps by someone, (h) all the tottering toward the bed on high heels, (i) all the sleeping with her face pressed into the pillow and her ass in the air, as she's been told she's slept since she was a baby.

•

That was how things would have been seventeen months ago. But this morning, *now*, is radically different. She drank practically nothing last night. She didn't kiss anyone. And she isn't sitting there with a cigarette in her hand either, because she stopped smoking about seventeen months ago, when she found out she was pregnant by the man who'd left her at a train station, and who had made her flash her tits so pathetically in protest. She's sitting in a hotel room that's spectacularly dull in terms of its decor, with a blue wall-to-wall carpet, and a narrow bed with white bed linen, and a chair with a reddish wooden frame and gray patterned fabric. And a TV, which is on: there are three huge walruses on the screen, diving down through greenish-blue water to the seabed to eat mussels. And Trine is sitting on the chair, with a cup of coffee, looking out at the back courtyard of the hotel, seeing nothing other than more windows to other rooms in the hotel. And her feet are cold and dry and bare, and she rubs them together, and feels how cold and dry they are, but can't be bothered to look for any socks to warm them up. And there's something disgusting about the fact that they're so dry, about the sound of her dry feet rubbing against each other; she had better stop rubbing them. The walruses start to dig around in the mud with their flippers, looking for mussels, and the water around them becomes cloudy.

6

Now, however, we're back on a January day ten years ago. And here we see Viggo (twenty-one at the time), who has just fallen off his bike, and we see one of his eyeteeth, which has been bothering him for a few years but has come loose in the past year since he had his root canal done and a gold tooth put in, fly through the air. It's 1998, and Viggo is cycling to his grandmother's funeral and has just collided in the most spectacular fashion with a bike stand, somersaulted over the handlebars, hit his jaw on a sign that says CUL-DE-SAC in such a way that his gold tooth loses its weak hold and flies through the air. And we follow the gold tooth's short flight through the air, then see it fall between two iron bars down into a drain in the gutter. And what happens to the tooth then is this: it is carried out to sea, via long underground canals. And there it is gobbled up by a salmon on its way to Greenland, who thinks it's found a rare delicacy. It will eventually end up on a fish counter, as the salmon will be caught. And there it will flash and catch the attention of someone who is going to be very important to Viggo, one January day ten years hence. But before that happens, it has to gleam in the belly of a salmon. And before that, Viggo has to fall off his bike. And all Viggo's external features—his pale, almost transparent eyes, his face, which, though pale, still looks dark, and his thick brown hair that falls down into his eyes—all combine to give an impression of intense pain. Ooowww! Viggo shouts and puts his hand to his face.

·

Viggo has been a reader all his life. A dreamer, a thinker, a lone wolf. Or perhaps a sheep, if the metaphorical animal ought to be more suited to Viggo's character. A lonely sheep, always on the fringes of the flock, wool a-trembling. As a child, strangely enough, his only friend was Ståle the thug, who always defended him, following an event that we'll come back to later, and this meant that Viggo was left in peace with his books at recess. It was only natural that Viggo should go on to study literature, given what he was like. It was only in literature that he found his soul mates. And peace. And if he took a course where everyone was studying literature, then surely he would find a real-life soul mate?

·

But no. When he moved away from home to study literature in Oslo, he immediately discovered that he didn't fit in there either. Largely because he didn't drink. He didn't drink! Because: oh, it's a long story, but okay: it's because Viggo absolutely believes in being true to oneself—that's why he doesn't drink alcohol. It's a personal belief that's helped him to weather being bullied at primary school and to deal with feeling lonely. And the feeling that he just had to go home the only time he tried to go to a party when he was sixteen and saw people who normally behaved in a certain way behaving in a completely different way as soon as they got drunk. They came over and hugged him and said that he was sweet, and it made him feel sick. Why couldn't they say that when they were sober? he thought and decided then and there *never* to drink. He was going to be true to who he was! Surely at some point he would meet someone who had the same feelings as he did, deep down? Someone who had escaped to the bike shed to read while the others played football? Someone who trembled too, someone who had days when they were so nervous that even the slightest sensory impression might knock them off-kilter—when, for instance, the densely patterned tights of the lady in front of them might make them rush to the nearest bush and throw up, because the tights made them so inexplicably anxious? Someone like him, who on days like that, when everything just went right in without any filter, might also, for example, come to believe, and most vehemently, that a box of matches or a paper clip lying on a desk was about to explode?

•

But so far, it hadn't happened! And then one day when he was sitting in a lecture theater at the University of Oslo, the female lecturer, who was talking about Kafka's *The Castle*, Viggo's favorite book other than Dante's *Divine Comedy*, was so nervous and was sweating so much that she drew a kind of Hitler mustache on herself when she touched her upper lip with two fingers covered in whiteboard marker smudges, to the delight and concealed sniggers of his non-soul-mates, and Viggo found himself taken aback. Here was someone who was just as nervous as he was when faced with the world. He sweated like that too when he was nervous! And all his life, people had whispered and sniggered about him as well.

·

He went up to her during the break, even though he wouldn't normally dare, and said, with dry mouth and sweating brow, that she should perhaps wipe off the mustache. What mustache? she asked, and looked at him, confused, and she noticed how beautiful he was, this fumbling student, and what incredible eyes he had. That one, he said, and pointed at the whiteboard pen smudges left on her upper lip by her two fingers. He hadn't meant to touch her lip. But he did, with his fingertip. And in that fingertip-touching moment, a curious bond was created between them. Or, he *believed* a curious bond was created. He believed it for the six months that the student and lecturer met for sex and conversations in tutorial rooms and other out-of-the-way places, and in fact continued to believe it, even after the female lecturer said to him, "For me, it's over," then picked up her bag and left. As far as she was concerned, the fascination had waned, she'd moved on. And in any case, she was forty, and didn't have time to get involved in a deep relationship; her great love was literature, a conclusion she'd reached over time, with some degree of suffering, but of which she was absolutely convinced. But it was his conviction as well! Love, literature. She neglected to say that his nervousness was starting to annoy her, the fact that he sometimes thought things would explode even though he knew they wouldn't, the constant soul-searching and fumbling, that he never made any suggestions about what they should do, that he obviously worshipped her—all of which she found problematic: in short, she'd simply had enough. He'd called a brilliant quote from Camus's *The Myth of Sisyphus* after her when she picked up her bag, put it over her shoulder, and walked down the corridor, having said what she had to say about their relationship: *There are no frontiers between the disciplines that man sets himself for understanding and loving. They interlock, and the same anxiety merges them!* but: no response. Viggo stood in the corridor and felt his insides being torn to shreds, she was his first and only love, he'd finally found solidarity, an internal solidarity. But he understood well enough, without her having to say it. She'd had enough of him. His trembling wool. He had to hide his face in his beautiful, but oh so useless, hands.

•

Viggo is now standing by his grandmother's grave, and he looks at his hands as the coffin is lowered into the ground. Through me [you pass] into eternal pain! pops into his mind. Those brackets, by the way, have been added to show that he's remembering the quote incorrectly, but that *we* have remembered it correctly, and we wanted to point out the discrepancy: the brackets don't appear in his mind, no, he just thinks it all, bracket-free, accidentally replacing "you pass," as the line should read, with *it passes*. But: no, no, he mustn't think that, Grandma's not going to hell, why did that quote have to pop up right now? The quote, which is engraved on the gates of hell in Dante's *Divine Comedy*, his favorite work other than Kafka's *The Castle*, has been on Viggo's mind all day. He read it very early this morning, when he was sitting on the plane waiting for it to take off and take him home, to the funeral, he sat there and read the inscription written in capital letters as the throbbing of the engine intensified: THROUGH ME [YOU PASS] INTO ETERNAL PAIN! He snapped the book shut. He thought: Is it symbolic? Is it the plane? Is he going to pass into eternal pain? Is the plane going to crash? Or is it *he himself* that's the problem, the self of himself, is that the gate to hell?

•

Because what had he done, following the unhappy ending of his relationship with the female lecturer with a razor mind? He had partied, he who never drank. One day three weeks ago, the day after the female lecturer had said that it was over, he had bumped into Ståle, the friendly thug from his childhood, down by the law school in the center of town, and Ståle had shouted *fuck, man*, is that you! And Viggo had replied in his usual awkward way *yes it* (and then mumbled "is" as quietly as he could, since he'd realized that he should have stopped at "yes" and that instead of "yes," he should really have said "yeah"). And then they had hugged each other, or rather, Ståle had embraced Viggo, and Viggo had given Ståle a couple of careful pats on the back. Fuck, man, Ståle said again, after all these years, what are you up to? What are you doing in Oslo? I thought you'd end up as a librarian and part-time shepherd. I'm studying literature, Viggo said. Fuck, man, Ståle said, and laughed out loud, of course you're studying literature. Ståle was studying economics at the business school, and thanks to this chance meeting of these two childhood conspirators at Universitetsplassen, Viggo had ended up in the random circle that always surrounded Ståle. Only this time he didn't sit in the bike shed. We should catch up, Ståle said, let's go out this evening, we have to! Fuck, man! And Viggo simply thought, with a kind of universally resigned sigh: why not. Why not, given the state of things?

•

And as he stands at his grandmother's grave, looking at his hands, the past three weeks of blurred Ståle chaos slowly dissipate, the way that mud in water sinks and settles. The mud: he'd partied with Ståle for three weeks. He had drunk drinks that he hadn't even known existed. He had pulled small umbrellas out of olives. He had talked to people he'd never have believed he would talk to. He had danced on the dance floor, even though he realized that he didn't dance very well and people were looking at him and laughing, and he had thought, why not, *why not!* Why not live fast and loose and unwind out of oneself? He had tried as *best* he could, to unwind out of himself. And then his grandma died. As though the universe was telling him: *everything that is you is now dying.* Through me, he thinks, you pass into eternal pain. That was what he'd done! With his relationship with the female lecturer and all the partying afterward, he'd gone through the gates of hell. He'd not been true to himself. In fact, Dante's words didn't allude to the gates of hell at all, Viggo thinks to himself as he stands there in front of the grave. They allude to one's own actions. The *me* in this. What is the *me* in him? The *me* in him was the trembling. The trembling that made him fall for the lecturer, the trembling that made him agree to party with Ståle, the pathetic attempt to unwind himself out of his shell. But is a person's trembling enough to cast them into hell? Viggo wonders as he watches the coffin disappear into the ground. Can a person not tremble without being eternally damned?

7

And now we hear a flapping sound: it's Sigrid, she sits there pulling her lower lip down, then releasing it so it slaps against the upper lip, just as Sofia Coppola says "We're going to the production office" to the man who's filming her for the film about making *Lost in Translation*. We see Sofia Coppola walk toward a building and go up some steps at the same time that we hear the sound of Sigrid's bottom lip slapping against her top lip. Sigrid is watching the behind-the-scenes documentary about *Lost in Translation*, she's looking for the scene where Charlotte wanders around the hotel room in an oversized man's shirt. Despite the oversized man's shirt, she *loves* this film. Magnus also loves the film. She sometimes wonders if it's Scarlett Johansson, the actress who plays Charlotte, that Magnus loves and not the film itself and then she feels utterly demoralized, because she's nothing like Scarlett Johansson. Her breasts, for example, aren't half as big. Not even a fifth. When they first started to grow, she would stand in the shower and gaze at her tiny breasts and look forward to them getting bigger, but they never did. It was one of the biggest disappointments in Sigrid's life. She stood in the shower as a thirteen-year-old, as a fourteen-year-old, as a fifteen-year-old, as a sixteen-year-old, as a seventeen-year-old, and thought: when I'm eighteen, they'll be bigger than they are now. But when she stood in the shower as an eighteen-year-old, her breasts were just as small as they had been when she was thirteen. There was nothing she could do but accept it! She's told Magnus about it. And now she's sitting there flapping her bottom lip against her top lip as she watches the film about making *Lost in Translation* because she thinks that Sofia Coppola might say something about the choice of costumes for the film in general, and more specifically: about the oversized man's shirt, but instead is astonished to discover that Sofia Coppola is very like the main character in her own film, except that Sofia Coppola is even more vague and whimsical, and she doesn't have such big breasts as Scarlett, they might even be smaller than Sigrid's (which pleases Sigrid intensely). But Sigrid thinks that having such tiny vanishing tits actually suits her really well, as there's something ethereal about Sofia Coppola. When she talks, the sound barely manages to carry through her lips and past her big teeth, and when she walks, it's like she glides rather than walks. The most recent thing that Sigrid has heard about Sofia Coppola is that she's pregnant, and she wonders how it's possible for a pregnant woman to glide sublimely across the floor! Here on the computer screen in front of her, however, Sofia Coppola is sitting up thin as a straight line and smiling an ever-so-faint and disarming smile, telling us this is her *dream*, she almost can't believe that Bill Murray really is coming today, and she can't wait to see him, she says, sitting on the bed in a kimono, looking sad. It's quite incredible how similar Sofia Coppola is to her lead character, they've even got almost the same hair, and the clothes she's wearing are the same muted, almost fading colors. She has to ring Magnus about it, she thinks. No, she has to resist. No, she's got to call him! No, she *must* resist.

•

Hello, Magnus says, she can hear that he's walking somewhere outside, with cars whizzing by. Hello, Sigrid says. How's things? she asks. You know, Magnus says. Did you have a good time in Prague? she asks. Yeah, Magnus says. I'm watching a film about the making of *Lost in Translation*, Sigrid tells him, and do you know what, Sofia Coppola is just like Scarlett! Or perhaps not physically, because her breasts aren't as big. She's actually got quite small—but very nice—breasts. There's no answer. Hello? Sigrid says. Hello, yes, I'm here, Magnus says. Oh, I thought you'd left me here to talk about Sofia Coppola's tits on my own. Magnus laughs. But it's actually quite strange, Sigrid continues, it's as if she's directed herself in a way, which is pretty amazing, if for example you think about the opening shot where Charlotte is lying with her back to the camera, and we only see part of her back and her butt down to her knees, and she's wearing see-through panties, and the title appears in three separate words, first "*Lost*," and then "*in*," over her bum, and then "*Translation*," farther down, and the way they seem to glide onto the screen and then fade and disappear; it's *just* like Sofia Coppola! I'm blown away, Sigrid says, to think that even the way the opening credits are used can give a perfect picture of inner life.

Mmm, Magnus says. Great, he says. Sigrid collapses back in her chair. He's not interested! Where are you off to? she asks. I've got an audition for the radio orchestra, I'll call you back later, he says. I'm glad you had a good time in Prague, Sigrid says. Mmm, Magnus replies.

•

But it is amazing, Sigrid tries to reason with herself as she sits there feeling cut off and rejected, stupid and geeky and incapable of understanding that other people are interested in different things, and that she should have stopped and tried to work out what that was before she just steamrollered on. But the way the title of the film has been designed is fantastic, and the director's way of being is fantastic. And the fact that they're the same. But there's no point. The only thing she feels now is a paralyzing sense of self. Why does she have to be like that?

•

The Belgian literary theorist Paul de Man stretches out his arm from the wall, puts his finger under her chin, and lifts her head. Pah! Sigrid says.

8

Thank you very much, says the host, a man in his fifties in a navy suit and a white shirt. He gives Kåre a handshake that's as heartfelt and firm as he's learned they should be. And then there's that slightly awkward pause, as always, when the applause has stopped and you've shaken hands, and you have to gather up everything you had with you, your jacket and bag, then leave the stage and the room as you notice that a couple of women in the front row are following you with their eyes. Kåre smiles to himself as he emerges into the corridor outside the conference suite. It's incredible, he thinks, just how unabashed some of these women are. He remembers the time when he was at a similar seminar a few years ago and a woman in the front row sat there licking her lips in a very deliberate manner. That is to say, she kept touching a particular point on her upper lip with her tongue as she stared up at him, and he got hotter and hotter under the collar as he stood there reading. Kåre doesn't even think that, given the situation, she might perhaps have had something wrong with her lip that was irritating her, maybe a crack that she wanted to moisten with her tongue so it didn't get any deeper, or maybe she was remembering that she'd left her lip balm on the bedside table at home and was feeling a bit desperate because she just couldn't survive a whole day without lip balm, and so was sitting there wondering where she might get some, whether they'd sell it at a news kiosk or if she'd have to go to the nearest supermarket, if she'd have to use her entire coffee break to go and buy lip balm instead of mingling, and wasn't listening to what Kåre was saying at all, but only keeping her eyes on him out of politeness—Kåre simply didn't consider this possibility, he thought it was outright flirting, good God, she's flirting with me, he thought, and now he's standing in the corridor outside the conference suite, thinking how glad he is that he's changed. If it had been pre-Wanda, there's no doubt what he would have done with the woman who'd sat there licking her lip.

•

But then there was Wanda. He'd seen her at John Dee's. She was the bass player in an up-and-coming underground band. She looked like she was more than six feet tall as she stood there on the stage, and she had thin black hair with straight bangs cut just above her eyebrows. Sometimes, when she looked up, it was as though she was looking straight up at her bangs, and was observing the audience through her own personal black curtain, her eyes narrow slits. She was wearing a black vest and tight black trousers and had long, muscular arms. She played the bass guitar in the sexiest and most aggressive manner that he'd ever seen anyone play it. He was there with one of the women whose head he'd touched, but

then, at the sight of this being with her bass, who played as
though she had the same sort of sex drive and aggression and
devil-may-care musicality in her as he had in him—albeit a
tender devil-may-care attitude—he was unable to concentrate
on anything else, and the woman he was with noticed that he
wasn't listening to anything she said, and that his mouth
missed the glass when he tried to take a drink of beer,
because he was staring at the bassist so intently. The woman
he was there with went home. And he just stood unmoving,
and thought, as he stared at the bassist: she is the ultimate
woman.

•

And now it was over. After three years with the ultimate
woman. What had gone wrong? Kåre walks out of Hotel
Norge onto Torgallmenningen, the main square. Bergenites
hurry past the statue of Ole Bull, who stands playing his vio-
lin on top of a small boulder, with no water around it. It's an
ordinary January morning, and mothers with buggies and
strollers, hip-hoppers with pimples and breaking voices,
businessmen with open jackets and yellow ties are all making their way to different destinations, at their normal speed.
Bergenites, Kåre thinks, are not half as well-dressed as Oslo
folk. He feels he stands out. He walks over to the record shop
to see if they're open yet, and feels very conspicuous in the
cityscape with his down jacket, Adidas shoes, and Skullcandy earphones. He feels that people are staring at him.
Kåre wonders if perhaps they recognize him from the newspaper; maybe there aren't *that* many authors living in Bergen?

9

Linnea is still standing with her sweater in her hands by the window in Copenhagen. She should really get a move on: Robert is sitting in his room waiting. It's today that she and Robert are going to the Ny Carlsberg Glyptotek to find the place where her main character is wandering around the Egyptian collection and suddenly meets a man. The film version of Göran, obviously. Who she, the real Linnea, hopes will be standing there, the real version, waiting for her when she comes in. At ten o'clock. On January 10, exactly two years after they first met. Because she, inspired by the films *Before Sunrise* and *Before Sunset*, which thankfully he had never seen, suggested that they shouldn't have any contact with each other, but that they should come back here in two years' time and meet again. Admittedly, in the films *Before Sunrise* and *Before Sunset*, Ethan Hawke and Julie Delpy actually meet ten years after their first, breathtaking encounter (they were originally only going to wait a year, but there were complications with a dead grandmother, and suddenly ten years had passed).

Linnea thought that waiting ten years was perhaps a bit too long, she couldn't guarantee that she wouldn't meet someone else in that time, and it also struck her that in ten years' time, Göran would actually be fifty-seven. Which was perhaps a little too old. So she said: maybe in two years' time we can come back to Copenhagen and see what happens? On January 10 at ten o'clock, two years from now. Göran had smiled and said: maybe. Who knows.

•

They had met at the Glyptotek, quite by accident. Göran, a professor in comparative literature at the University of Uppsala (who at this moment is waking up from his dream about the rattling keys), was in Copenhagen to give a lecture on epic poetry, his speciality, but right then was standing in the Glyptotek staring thoughtfully down at two Egyptian mummies lying side by side in a glass display case. She herself had come to Copenhagen in an attempt to throw herself into life, into the world, to feel that she was alive, having broken up with a boyfriend who had had sex with a barmaid two weeks before they were due to get married—but it had to be Europe, because the rest of the world seemed to be alarmingly un-Western, and preferably Scandinavia, as the rest of Europe seemed to be alarmingly un-Scandinavian— and then, suddenly, there she was, wandering around the fantastic displays of ancient art in the Glyptotek, which her mother had said on the phone she simply *must* visit.

•

Göran has not, like Linnea, seen his inner life reflected in the play of light of a chandelier, but he has, on the other hand, over the course of his forty-seven years, had similar personal epiphanies when looking at pictures of deserts, where the infinite expanses of sand seem to stretch endlessly toward an invisible horizon, like an hourglass on its side where time has stopped indefinitely. Sand—he could feel the deserts when he slipped under the surface in the bath at home in Sweden, when his wife and children and books and student assessments fell away under the water and all he could hear was the quiet hum of his own brain. When his hair started to go white at the age of thirty, he'd thought that it was like sand, white sand stealing up from his brain and into his hair, and within a few years, there was white sand all over his head, all over his face. And as Göran stood lost in these thoughts of sand, which at some point must have covered the two mummies in the glass display case in front of him, Linnea came into the room. She started, well almost, at the sight of another person. And in the dark blue, dimly lit room with mummies standing behind glass in every direction, and two mummies lying on the floor in a glass display case, this person seemed to be so alive and tangible. He had short white hair and a short white beard, but his eyebrows were still dark and heavy, and he looked up at her as though she was something far off on a distant horizon, like something he almost couldn't see, and the way he then looked down at the glass display case again, having done little more than register her presence, made him incredibly attractive, Linnea thought. He looked as though he was carrying the weight of the world on his shoulders as he stood there. She wanted him to look at her again. It's possible that this was what made him so attractive to her: that he was carrying the weight of the world behind those dark eyebrows, and in some way the weight of the world was highly attractive, in contrast to the lightness of the world, which could allow someone to sleep with someone else only two weeks before that someone was due to get married. The weight of the world *is* more solid, something that can anchor you to the surface of the earth, something you can hang on to, when all the world's winds are blowing with all their might, as they sometimes do. And then there was the fact that he barely seemed to notice her. He had to notice her!

•

But Göran had noticed her, that she came into the room with her fair, tousled hair and thin, delicate soul, and that she looked at him with big eyes, and that she walked around the room looking at the mummies that were displayed along the walls, while he just stayed where he was standing. She wasn't to know that he'd noticed her presence in an almost physical way, but also, it has to be said, in a symbolic way, as he was a professor of literature with a strong desire to find symbolic structures: here they were, two *living* people, in this room, man and woman, and there, in the glass case, lay they, two long-dead people, man and woman. She eventually stopped on the other side of the glass display case, filled with an intense, childish desire to be seen; she stood directly opposite him, and looked down at the two embalmed figures with their silent, painted faces. He lifted his eyes from the painted faces and looked at her (she felt herself tremble inside, tremble!): beautiful, he said in an (oh so) deep and hoarse voice. Yes, she said, in a voice that was very dry.

10

The inclusion of this scene by the glass display case in Linnea's film, however, bothers her producer, Robert. Has she, little Linnea, experienced it, in real life? Has she stood like that, by a glass display case containing two mummies, with an older man, and was there a magnetic sexual attraction? And now, thinking of Linnea in the shirt that looked like it belonged to a man, it bothers him even more. But what bothers Robert even more than that, to an excruciating degree, in fact, is the fact that this film is never going to happen. They haven't raised the last millions needed, even though he's told her they have. They haven't. He has kept her in the dark for a month now, since they were turned down. And it bothers him terribly as he sits in his hotel room in front of his Mac, looking at the severed horse head that someone found in a dump in Fitjar, which he came upon accidentally as he clicked around nervously because he had to do something while he waited. He is fully, and impeccably, dressed: he's wearing new Italian shoes, and he's had breakfast and will soon meet Linnea down in the reception area to take a taxi to the Glyptotek, and now he's sitting here reading about a severed horse head on *Bergens Tidende*'s website. Today is the day he must tell her that the film will never be made. It's a bit late to tell her now, as he's given Linnea the impression that the finances are in place, that he's managed to raise the missing millions in addition to the money he's already put on the table for her, from his own pocket. But he can't bear the thought of upsetting her. And why is that? Why can't a rich film producer bear the thought of upsetting a young, female film director, and how can a film producer bear to keep up a ridiculous farce in which he's fooled the staff in his production company into believing that he's working on a unique project that will also be very lucrative in the future, and that he wants exclusive rights to the work because the director is so special and fragile, how can he bear to carry on with it, as all it entails is endless false and reassuring smiles to his left and right as he makes his way to his office, where he can close the door and his eyes at the same time and feel how stiff his neck is? How can a film producer push this deception so far that he actually goes to Copenhagen with the film director he's kept in the dark to find locations for filming a pretend film, because it's a pretend film that's never going to be made and will just end up hanging, dangling stupidly in the air with all its arms and legs like a paper jumping jack when you pull the string? Let's be brief: because he's in love. Because Robert the film producer, for the first time in his fifty-one years of life, which have been filled exclusively with work, work, work and ambition, long days in suits, a deep passion for film, and better and better views from his office over the years, is so in love that he doesn't know what he's doing anymore. Linnea is the most exquisite thing he's ever seen. Or perhaps it's simply that he's never met anyone so exquisite before, because that's what she is: exquisite. He didn't know that the word "exquisite" existed before he saw her. But when he saw her, the word welled up from deep inside. E x q u i s i t e. Linnea is exquisite, with her light, delicate feyness and big, shining, yes, shining eyes, and it's so easy to understand why precisely the word "exquisite" emerged from deep within, without warning, the first time Robert saw her. She gave him the need both to crush her against him and to lift her gently up from the ground like a feather. And when he read the scene with the mummies, he felt a heat in his belly: might the fact that she, this exquisite young woman, could write such a scene, where there is a magnetic attraction between a younger woman and an older man, indicate that she was attracted to older men? And he was, with his fifty-one years, an older man. Maybe she could be attracted to him; this was one of the underlying thoughts that made Robert especially interested in the screenplay, which was basically about an unresolved relationship between a young woman and an older man. But now, even as he dreams about things like crushing her to him, the plot has started to bother him. Is it something she's experienced? Robert has never been any good at recognizing symbolism, or, for that matter, interpreting anything at all, really—he still feels a slight discomfort whenever he hears the name Ibsen—but somehow with Linnea's manuscript it's slowly dawned on him: the mummies, the symbolism of the mummies: is it some kind of vile joke? He would rather not believe that.

But, well. Because he dreams of such banal—but, for those who long for them, unachievable—things, such as a crushing embrace, lifting Linnea up gently from the ground as though she were a feather, holding her close at night, whispering in her ear, through her hair . . . because of all of this, and because he dreams of the moment when she'll say, with shining eyes, that she loves him, and that she's loved him since day one, and that it doesn't matter that her film will never be made. But, well. Because of all of this, he hasn't said anything. But today it will happen. Only he hasn't decided in which order it should happen. Confronting her about the film first or about his love. What would be best? Oh, *best*, he, Robert (fifty-one), has to hide his face in his hands, what would be least heart-explodingly nerve-wracking and awful is the question! He looks at the horse head minus its body. Light pink flesh hangs around its muzzle, which is peeled back in a loathsome grin.

•

Are you sure this is what you want, Robert? He feels nervousness gnawing an aching hole in his stomach. He takes his hands away from his face and tries to nod to his reflection in the window, but only sees the air outside. An unbelievable view, with long gray airplane bodies gliding through the atmosphere, but no face, no confirming nod, to himself.

11

Viggo looks around. His whole family is here, his father, his mother, his sister—when he sat together with them on the pew, he felt what he always feels when he's with his family: that they don't know each other. Or, that is to say, the three others know each other, but none of them really know him. His mother gave him a handkerchief, his father shook his hand and offered his condolences, and Viggo offered his condolences back, his sister gave him a hug. And now they're all standing around a hole in the ground and the coffin is being lowered into it. But who's she, standing there at the edge of the group, with a small, serious face, and a slightly too large black coat with turned-up sleeves? She looks about twelve and is very cute—he registers without really thinking. She looks anxious, like she's standing there hoping no one will notice that she's standing there, because she doesn't really belong there. Who is she? How did she know my grandma? Viggo thinks. Everyone standing here around the hole in the ground weeping knew my grandma, but I've never seen her before, and it feels like she knows it, the way she looks up, meets my eyes, then quickly looks at the ground again, keeps her eyes firmly on the ground as she lifts her foot and steps back, as if she's preparing to run because she's been discovered. But. She stays where she is. But she doesn't look up again. How did she know my grandmother? Viggo thinks. He's completely forgotten about the gates of hell. She stands there looking uncomfortable and a little lost in her big black coat. How sweet she is. I'll ask her, he thinks as they wander back to the chapel in a tight black flock for the post-funeral reception in the basement of the chapel, how she knows her. Then maybe she won't feel like an outsider anymore.

•

How, Viggo asks the little girl, in 1998, and doesn't tremble much at all, as she's only twelve, how, he asks, when he's finally made his way over to where she's standing at the edge of the chapel basement and has had time to take a few sips of pop from her glass and chat to one of his great-uncles, did you know my grandma? I used to bring her fish every Wednesday, she says. I'm the fishmonger's daughter. Dad said I should come, because he has to look after the shop. Oh, Viggo says. So that's the explanation. But, the girl says to Viggo, is that blood in the corner of your mouth? Have I got blood in the corner of my mouth? he asks, and presses the handkerchief he was given by his mother to his lips. I fell off my bike, he says. I fell off my bike and lost a tooth. He opens his mouth to show her, hooking his lip with a finger so the big, dark hole in his gum appears, and she thinks it's disgusting, his lip pulled back like that, all dry and stretched, and the pink gum and the hole between two teeth. Horrible, she says, about the fact that he's fallen off his bike and hurt himself, but also, as far as she's concerned, about the horrible sight of him pulling back his lip, like you would with a horse, she thinks, revealing the gross horse's mouth behind its great muzzle. Where's your tooth now, then? she asks. Have you got it in your pocket? It fell down a drain in the gutter, he says. I heard a plop and it was gone. Really? the girl exclaims. Yep, he says. I had a tooth pulled out a couple of days ago, the girl tells him, and opens her mouth wide, so he can see. How strange, he thinks, that I'm standing here at Gran's funeral, staring into the mouth of a twelve-year-old girl. He can see her uvula, which hangs like a disgusting fleshy polyp at the top of her throat, and her small tongue, which is healthy and pink, but he can barely see any missing tooth. Maybe if you pull your tongue back into your mouth I'll be able to see the hole properly, Viggo suggests. Oh, the girl laughs, I thought it would be best to open wide, the way I open wide at the dentist. She pulls her tongue back up toward the roof of her mouth and points to a hole on her lower jaw. Her mouth smells of raspberries. He inspects the hole in her mouth. Yes, I can see it now, he says. She closes her mouth and looks at him, then smiles sheepishly. He's overwhelmed by her sweetness, and her smallness and her trust; the fact that she stood with her mouth open for him and now feels a little ashamed makes him feel calm. The fact that she's not learned to control her impulses yet is charming, he thinks, and wants to stroke her hair. It's fair, flat, and flyaway, girl's hair, the kind of hair that doesn't know it's hair yet, and now he's moved, but he doesn't pat her.

12

Sigrid has her head on her arms on her desk and is thinking. She has to change. She has to toughen up. She has to stop analyzing everything and stop being so caught up in things that she forgets all else around her, and she has to stop thinking that people are all interested in the same things as her. Because they're not! They're not, Paul de Man, she says, and presses his nose with her finger. Naturally, Paul de Man doesn't answer: after all, he's Belgian, and a photograph.

•

But there's a cry inside Sigrid. Somewhere deep inside her body there's a cry, which if it were to be replicated in color and not sound would be painted sheer black, the kind of darkness that might exist in a universe without stars. If it were a sound, you probably wouldn't hear it, even though it's loud, more like a howl, as it would still be locked up, as though inside a mountain. It's the cry of loneliness. At this very moment, that cry of loneliness cries out in Sigrid, and any second now she'll bawl her eyes out. Because she really *did* think that the way the title appeared in the film was fantastic, and that it really was like Sofia Coppola herself. Or like how she seems to be, at least. Sofia Coppola *can't* be any different. It *is* interesting that surfaces and depths are inherent in each other. It *is* interesting, and important, that it's possible to express something about your deepest depths in these ways. Just as Sofia Coppola has managed to do, Sigrid thinks. In just the way that she herself so clearly hasn't managed to do! Oh, the cry of loneliness, the cry of loneliness, stuck in her throat like a great, fat lump!

•

Tears well up in her eyes. No, enough! She stands up with a shudder and makes a point of wiping her eyes in an affected, exaggerated manner. She's going to write a letter to Sofia Coppola, that's what she'll do. *She* will understand what Sigrid means. She looks at the photograph of Kåre Tryvle on the table. And you, she thinks. She has a feeling that Kåre Tryvle would understand it all. Kåre Tryvle—she wonders whether Kåre Tryvle is thin, or whether he's got some weight to him, like Bill Murray. And whether it would feel like she was being absorbed when he held her in his arms and said: I understand *exactly* what you mean. Into her hair. With lips that she: kisses. Then they look deep into each other's eyes, and then they kiss again. Oh arms, arms, *the arms* that would hold her tight and hug her so she didn't need to think about a thing!

•

Concentration. She writes: "Dear Sofia Coppola. I've seen your movie *Lost in Translation*, and I love it. I'm writing an article about women and surfaces and I have a question about

surfaces that I would like to ask you; I feel that surfaces are
very important in your movie. Not in a shallow way, but in
a profound way. For instance, the opening scene where Charlotte lies on the bed and the title appears almost like in a
dream"—she stops, because she suddenly knows that she's
never going to send this letter, and that if she did send it, she
would never get an answer. And besides, it would take too
long for the letter to get to the United States and for the answer to come back; her deadline is in three days! And besides
that, she doesn't know *where* to send it. And besides that
again, she didn't really like the formulation "almost like in a
dream," it's too whimsical and poetic, she scores it out, so the
letter she's never going to send ends with just "and the title."

•

But the concluding sentence irritates her, the fact that she
can't think of anything to say other than "almost like in a
dream." She tries again: "And the title appears as if you were
looking inside someone's distant mind, and the words were the
stray thoughts appearing and disappearing as if they had nowhere to go"—but that's probably not grammatically correct
either: "and the title appears as if you were looking inside" has
to be formulated in a different way, but in what way? "And
the title gives the impression of looking into," "And the title
appears in a way that gives me the impression of looking into
someone's mind"? It strikes her: Should there be a possessive
apostrophe in "someone's"? Or is it written "someones"? And
what's more, it's not correct that these thoughts "had nowhere to go," or at least that's not the first impression you get!
The main impression is that they appear only to disappear
again, kind of like when you're sitting on a train looking out

the window and listening to music, and thoughts just drift in and out of your head, it's more *that* kind of feeling, that something appears for just long enough for you to register its existence, and *that's* the feeling she has after seeing Sofia Coppola's transparent, vague way of talking and being, "And the title appears in a way that gives me the impression of looking into someone's mind." And now there's the question of genitive apostrophe! Was her memory of English grammar really that bad? She deletes the whole sentence and starts again: "For instance, the opening scene, where Charlotte lies on the bed and the title—"

13

Kåre walks along Torgallmenningen. What had happened between him and Wanda, Kåre thinks, looking up at the houses on Mount Fløyen as he walks in the January light that feels as though it's staring down the hill over the city from behind Nygårdshøyden, was that he *was* capable of hurting the person he loved the most. He would never have believed that, back then when he stood at the concert looking up at Wanda, who was playing as though she, the bass guitar, and her black bangs were the only things that existed in the world. He would never get bored of her, he would always look up to her. But alas, he thinks grimly, and looks up at the small wooden houses that seem to huddle together up over the slope toward Fløyen.

•

Explanation: the admission that he was the kind of man who could hurt the person he loved the most was rooted in something that had taken seed in him after the almost equally unbelievable argument that he and Wanda had had after watching *Kill Bill: Vol. 2* one evening a week ago. The discussion might have seemed rather trivial on the surface, as it wasn't about them at all, but about Uma Thurman's character, the Bride, in *Kill Bill: Vol. 2*, but it had, all the same, caused a green substance to ooze out from under the skin of what they'd considered to be their perfect, unified body. Kåre and Wanda had watched a DVD of *Kill Bill: Vol. 2* that evening, and when they went for a walk afterward, they started to talk about the film, even though they had a policy never to talk about films immediately after they'd seen them, as they might then analyze the whole experience to death. In the case of *Kill Bill: Vol. 2*, they had initially agreed that it was very different from *Kill Bill: Vol. 1*, they had both enthused about the way in which Quentin Tarantino had highlighted the East-West issue by making the first film more Eastern, with lots of kung fu, etc., and the second more like a kind of spaghetti-western version of the revenge wreaked by Uma Thurman's character. So far everything was fine and dandy, discussing the film. They were almost buoyed by the fact that they were walking where they were, along the river, and discussing a film they'd just watched. Wanda blew her bangs to the side and looked over at him with a small smile. Kåre took her hand and gave it a squeeze. And when Kåre said "that scene with the pregnancy test was fantastic," they both burst out laughing at the thought of Uma Thurman the contract killer and her own contract killer, in turn, fumbling with the pregnancy test that Thurman had just taken and discovered was positive at the exact moment when her contract killer attempted to kill her by shooting through the door. It was then, after all their laughter, that Wanda said something that sparked the argument. It started innocently enough: all she said was that she thought the whole motherhood question was a bit problematic. The film plot was simple enough: The Bride was supposed to kill Bill, her true love, whom she'd left, and who'd shot her through the head when she was heavily pregnant and about to marry someone else. In film number one, on the other hand, Wanda said, neither Bill nor her daughter, B.B., as it turns out she's called in film number two—whom The Bride thought she'd lost when she was shot through the head by Bill, her boss, her great love and father of the child—neither of them was actually present in film one, and The Bride was the only main character. And she was strong and clear and motivated only by the thought of her revenge on Bill. But in number two, Wanda felt that the thrust of the film was skewed too much toward the fact that The Bride was *a mother*, in that not only did she have everything to lose when she found out that she was pregnant, but she also had nothing to lose when she thought she no longer had the child. That her actions, which in film one were clearly the actions of an extremely independent woman, no matter how violent they were, and it was so cool to have a female protagonist in a gangster film, now, in film number two, were *explained* and *rooted in* the über-typical female role: that of being a mother, and let's not forget, a woman who's been let down by her boyfriend! And, said Wanda—who was not a mother herself and had a somewhat strained relationship with young mothers with strollers in cafés (she would *never* do that if she ever became a mother, take a stroller to a café! she couldn't imagine herself pushing a stroller at all)—there was something odd about the relationship between The Bride and

Bill, the way in which, when their relationship was explained and shown in flashbacks, The Bride was somehow totally *inferior* to Bill, the way The Bride—I mean, *The Bride*!—was much younger than Bill, who was almost an *old* man, and she was made to look like a fourteen-year-old girl when she listened, full of admiration, to him telling one of his many stories. Jesus, it was unbelievable, Wanda exclaimed, who, in addition to being a super-sexy and aggressive bassist, had studied at university (which made her no less the ultimate woman in Kåre's eyes), it was unbelievable when you thought about it, Wanda said: Uma, the tough cookie who fought her way effortlessly through eighty-eight mad Japanese gangsters, was now lying there in the light of a bonfire—in such an *epic, archetypal situation*, no less!—with a smile of admiration on her face, listening to Bill's stories, making only occasional exclamations like "no" or "wow." That's not really what she said, is it, Kåre objected with a laugh; no, Wanda said, but it might as well have been. It was quite a statement the film made there, putting a man and a woman in such an epic, archetypal situation, the mother of all narratives: sitting around a fire listening to stories, and as usual it was the man who was telling and the woman who was listening. I mean, Wanda said with a scornful haha, just how *conventional* can you get? The whole film, which pretends to be the story of a strong woman, is in fact undermined by this.

14

Wanda, who uttered those words a week ago, is now walking through Frognerparken with her usual brisk, angry step, thinking, at the same time as Kåre, about the quarrel they'd had about *Kill Bill: Vol. 2*. She's wearing a gray tracksuit, with a light gray vest underneath, which is darker across her sweaty chest. Her black bangs lie in wet, wavy strips across her forehead, and her eyes are determined. It's cold, but Wanda doesn't give a damn.

•

The past week hasn't been easy for Wanda. She's tried, frantically, to keep her spirits up, gone to the studio and practiced alone, but it's been hard to hold her bass, it's been so hard to hit the strings with her fingers, it felt like there were no veins or sinews or muscles in her arms. She's stood in the bathroom at her mother's house, where she's staying, and looked at herself from under her black bangs, and noticed that her jaw suddenly looks incredibly square, as though her lips were pulling into her mouth, perhaps because she's constantly on the verge of tears. And she doesn't want to be. Better then to tighten your lips and have a square jaw. Better then to go to the studio and practice, better then to pull on your tightest trousers and lie on the floor while you zip them up, because that's the only way you can get them on, wriggle into the blackest snakeskin in your wardrobe, only to fail because you've put on weight without noticing, and so end up lying on the floor with a pair of tight jeans halfway up your thighs, and instead light a cigarette, since you can just about manage from this position to get hold of the pack on the floor by the bed. Lie on the floor of your childhood bedroom after another unsuccessful attempt to get it together, and smoke and look up at the ceiling and try not to cry.

Sorry, kiddo, but you thought wrong!

She had *known* when she saw that scene! Her stomach ached as she sat there on the sofa with Kåre and saw Bill and The Bride sitting opposite each other in the last big scene of the film. Bill had shot The Bride in the foot with a dart of truth serum, so The Bride would tell him the truth about everything, and now it was time for the final reckoning: Who would manage to kill the other first? These two, who loved each other so much. They sat opposite each other, and Uma Thurman said that even though she knew that Bill was the most ruthless of them all, she never thought he could do this, to *her*. And with a kind of apologetic tilt of the head, Bill said: I'm really sorry, kiddo, but you thought wrong. And Wanda wanted to scream. Because wasn't that exactly what she feared would happen to her too? That Kåre would leave/hurt her/ sleep with someone else/fall passionately in love with someone else/find someone who wasn't as morose as her? Yes. And the very thought, the fact that it was a possibility, now demonstrated on film, that someone could hurt someone else as much as Bill hurt The Bride, was unbearable. *Because hadn't she always had the feeling that Kåre was only hers on loan? That he was bound to break it off?* That he, who she—the toughest and most untouchable of all untouchables—had opened herself to and allowed herself to love more than anything in the world, would at some point hurt her in ways that would rob her of all her life force? Okay, it was only a movie and the plot and reactions were more exaggerated, more of a caricature, than what happened in real life, but its symbolic value held true for Wanda all the same. *This is something that happens.* It could happen. It could! And that was because: Kåre was like Bill. He'd done it before. He'd hurt absolutely all the women he'd ever been with before her, and all in more or less the same way, as he'd told her himself. He had told her about his cold heart, which she had warmed. What if it suddenly cooled again?

•

And now she's storming through the park, early on this January morning. She's got PJ Harvey playing in her ears, and it should come as no surprise to anyone that she's singing to herself in despair: "I'm scared baby! I wanna run! This world's crazy! Give me the gun!"

15

Always, Kåre thinks as he walks toward the record store, Wanda had to bring up the feminist perspective! The thing with the relationship between The Bride and Bill is a gangster film trope, he'd told her as they walked along the river that evening, the boss's minions are *always* subservient, they always look blindly up to the boss, and sometimes they eventually have to kill the boss, which is the case with The Bride! She kills him! How do you get that to fit in with your feminist criticism? Kåre said, then added that she should appreciate that it was a major twist on this trope that a female was the most feared of all the minions, and that it was she who won in the end, plus the fact that she had a daughter who appeared to be as fearless as her mother, as they lay there on the bed in a hotel room and watched *Shogun Assassin*! And Kåre actually thought that it was good that The Bride was a mother, that rather than confirming conventions, it was turning them on their head, because what mother would allow her five-year-old daughter to watch a film filled with cold-blooded

murders carried out by callous hands? But more than anything, Kåre thought, keeping quiet at first, what was *really*
bothering Wanda was that she was jealous of Uma Thurman.
Because she knew that the only women that Kåre could
stand were strong women, he couldn't bear uncertainty and
hesitation, and that she herself, Wanda, was one of the stron-
gest people Kåre knew, and that was part of his attraction and
love for her. And she liked that, because she *was* strong. But
she had a flaw too, and that flaw was her jealousy. And it was a
tragic paradox, Kåre thought—the very fact that she was at-
tacking Uma Thurman's character for being the image of a
subservient woman in fact only revealed her own uncertainty
and lack of confidence. Because hadn't she gone all weird and
grumpy when he'd clicked on an interview with Uma Thurman on the *Dagbladet* website after he'd already read an interview with her in *VG* when the film first came out? Yes.
"What's with the Uma Thurman obsession?" *"Obsession?
Because I've read two interviews with her?"* Yes, wasn't it a
bit obsessive to open an interview with this woman in *Dagbladet* when you'd just been reading about her in *VG*? Were
there any particular nuances in the *Dagbladet* interview that
he was pleased to discover? *Jesus*, could he not just look
around on the *Dagbladet* website without it meaning that he
was going to fly out to Hollywood and start a relationship
with the most desirable actress in the world? *Jesuuus!!* And it
certainly didn't improve her mood when he said that she was
just jealous because Uma was so blonde and beautiful, and
Wanda said that this was the stupidest thing she'd ever heard.
Until she, having sulked for the entire day and walked ag-
gressively round Frognerparken in her sneakers with PJ Harvey

playing in her ears and cried in secret, then snuggled up to him on the sofa in the evening and asked if he didn't love her more because she'd been jealous of a film star he'd never meet? And that perhaps it wasn't about Uma Thurman, as such, but more about *the potential other woman*, who might suddenly appear from nowhere? I think, said Kåre as they walked along the river, it's about Uma Thurman. I think you're still jealous. Wanda turned toward him with a furious expression. What did you just say? She rounded on him, her eyes narrowed under her black bangs. You think this is about *jealousy*? Yes, I do, Kåre said. Fucking hell, Wanda said, you're fucking worse than Bill. You don't even believe I can think, you think I'm ruled by my bodily functions and emotions, any minute now you're going to ask if I'm premenstrual! You think I'm *worse* than Bill? Kåre shouted, because of that question, you think that I'm worse than someone who was prepared to kill his own girlfriend and unborn baby? *Aaaaaargh*, you know what I mean! Wanda shouted. No, I fucking well don't, Kåre said. And neither of them pushed the matter any further, Wanda threw up her hands and felt like her head was boiling, her stomach was boiling, with rage, Kåre imitated Wanda and threw up his hands, and was exasperated, fed up. They walked home in silence, but that made it even worse, perhaps, the fact that they didn't carry on arguing, but were silent, and that neither of them picked up where they'd left off or tried to do anything to end the silence, they were just totally and utterly silent. They were silent as they walked down the street toward the house, silent as they opened the door, silent as they walked up the stairs into the flat, they were silent as they ate separately, silent as they brushed their teeth separately, as they each lay down on their side of the bed, and silent as they fell asleep. And when Kåre woke up in the middle of the night and the room was dark and he looked at Wanda as she lay there asleep, he thought of a quote, but couldn't remember who had written it, where he'd read it: "How strange this will seem to you, when you no longer have this arm under your head," because that was the truth! He suddenly just knew it, as he lay there gazing at her sleeping face—that he would pull back his arm, that she would sleep without his arm under her head from now on. And he put his head down on his own pillow and looked up at the ceiling and felt icy cold inside. As though his heart had turned itself off. Click: darkness. As though it was irrevocable, too late. And he turned to the wall, closed his eyes, and fell asleep. When they woke up the next morning, everything had changed, they tried to be normal, but everything was abnormal, it was abnormal to eat breakfast and abnormal to say have a good day, abnormal to hug, their bodies were all kinds of stiff, and it was abnormal to come home again after he'd played golf, and in the end he and Wanda sat at the kitchen table and cried and said that perhaps they should take a break, she wanted to go back to her mother's for a week and then they would see. Hadn't they both felt that the relationship had been teetering on the edge for some time now? Yes. (Tears.) But he didn't feel much; all he felt, when he looked at Wanda standing there with puffy eyes, looking out the window, was nothing, even a kind of relief. He withdrew his arm. And she took her bass guitar and left. And *that* was what had bothered him for a whole week, that he was back in that old place again, that nothing made an impression, that he was just cold. So what he'd felt when he watched the scene where Bill says to The Bride that she's wrong had been right, he could do something like that to her, shoot her in the head. He'd felt like he'd been found out. He had it in him too!

•

The record shop isn't open yet. He decides to go and find somewhere he can have a coffee, his plane isn't until five, and he now regrets thinking that it might be good to look around another town before traveling back to Oslo and the state in which he left his life. And the state of his life, thinks Kåre, is that he feels nothing, even when faced with the ultimate woman.

•

He goes to Baker Brun, and as he orders a double espresso over a glass counter full of sugared buns filled with almond paste and vanilla cream, he thinks how *intensely* he dislikes pastries.

16

Drift, Sigrid says out loud. She's found the collection of Olav H. Hauge's poems on the bookshelf and opened the book at the poem she's marked by folding a corner of the page.

My life is drifting on the Arctic Ocean
My ship frozen in desolation.

Oh, that's just how she feels! She's twenty-three years old, and she's already a boat that's frozen in the ice. If this were a film, and she were some miserable, closed person, she thinks, something would happen at this point to pull her out of her reclusiveness. If she had braces and wore glasses, this would be the point where someone came along and taught her to wear contact lenses and makeup, and someone else would do her hair. If, at this point, she were a character who'd lived at home with her mother in a sixties-style flat all her life, something would happen to knock her existence out of orbit, her mother might die and she would have to take her odd, unfashionable self out into the world and go through all the changes that make a character interesting to follow on the silver screen. *But that's not reality!* Sigrid wants to shout. People just stay sitting in their rooms. They sit there, and nothing happens. They don't change, they just stay the same. Even if they're only twenty-three years old! They look things up in books, they have photographs of Belgian literary theorists on their wall, and they sigh heavily when they read something that makes them see the closed life they lead for what it is: closed. Perhaps they buy another type of yogurt one day, but come to the conclusion that Fruits of the Forest is the best flavor after all, and so go back to buying Fruits of the Forest yogurt. If she were going to make a movie, Sigrid thinks, it would be *exclusively* about a girl who sat in her room, and about what happened to her there, what she thought about, and how she went over to the skylight and looked out at the twin spires of St. Mary's Church and longed for something greater than life itself, which—alas—hadn't arrived quite yet, and so far showed no sign at all of ever arriving.

•

Through me, she writes. Where did that come from? Through me, an oversized man's shirt, they pass into eternal pain, these bare-legged women! Dante, of course, from the inscription on the gates of hell. Through me [they] pass into eternal pain. She finds Dante's *Divine Comedy* and finds the place where she thinks the quote comes from.

•

And it is indeed from Canto 3, on page 95 of Sigmund Skard's translation from 1965, published in paperback in 1994.

17

Sigrid sits there and imagines a whole line of women in over-sized men's shirts with bare legs, slightly hunched shoulders, and tousled hair filing through a gigantic stone gateway. It makes her laugh. She thinks that she would actually quite like a necklace like the one Charlotte's wearing in *Lost in Translation* as she pads around in her oversized man's shirt: a diamond crescent moon. A diamond crescent moon that shines in a quiet, intense way like her inner self. Because that's the thing about Charlotte. You can't quite get hold of her, but she shines, a bit like Sofia Coppola. And a bit like Sigrid as well. Because Sigrid shines too, as mentioned before, brightly, her inner light shines brightly too, only not many people have discovered it yet, her secret, sparkling light. If she had a necklace like that, she could wear it as a secret symbol for what she is and knows. That she herself shines. And the fact that it's a crescent moon makes it even more symbolic, it's not a full moon shining to its absolute maximum, only a small sliver of the moon that's illuminated, while the rest stays hidden in the dark. *That's the truth*, Sigrid thinks, and her eyes fill with tears. Her: a lot of her is still hidden in the dark. One day she will shine like a full moon, but for the time being, she's just a crescent. A nail clipping.

•

But what she wants most. Sigrid feels it sink through her. She feels Kåre Tryvle's arms around her, arms that hold and hold and hold her. I long for everything, Sigrid thinks, that's the truth. She longs for *that*. That which is everything. And which she hasn't experienced. And which she certainly will never experience with Magnus.

•

It gets darker and darker inside her body, darker and darker in her eyes, she has to open them and look at the computer. The screen has gone black, she sees her own reflection as a kind of ghostly face, with dark pools where her eyes, nose, and mouth—if she opens it—are. She picks up the book with Kåre Tryvle's face on it, his square face, the fine lines around his eyes, the dark hair turning gray at the temples, and his eyes that look like they understand what there is to understand about her, everything that Magnus doesn't understand, for example. To think that when he sat down to have his photograph taken, he looked into the camera, but what he was really looking at was Sigrid, someone who just happened to buy the book, someone who didn't know what she was doing in the bookshop until she picked out this particular book, randomly, and turned it over to look at the back cover and met the eyes of an author on a day when she had wandered around feeling that she was someone that no one saw. It had to be fate.

•

This is what she longs for, among other things, when she previously thought that she longed for everything. That he'd be able to feel it when she looked at the picture. That he'd be able to know that she knew. And that, unlike Magnus, he'd know how to appreciate it.

•

The cursor that sits there blinking is a narrow black line: What will happen, she suddenly thinks, given all she thought about earlier, if she doesn't write any of it down? Where will it go? Everything she thought and felt about Sofia Coppola, and the title that only just appears before it disappears again, thoughts and feelings that have floated through her and meant something to her and that she wanted to share with someone, but which (a) someone didn't have time to listen to, and (b) she hasn't been able to express to anyone yet. Will it all just slip back into the dark whence it came? If she's not able to express it?

•

This is also a substantial part of the everything she longs for. This yearning state she so often finds herself in!

•

Is she not a crescent moon after all? she wonders. Is she *complete* darkness? Is it her fate here in life never to be seen? And is the moon actually a good metaphor, as it has no light of its own, but just reflects the sun? On the other hand, though, couldn't it be said that—oh God, she's fallen into the sun-moon trap! She's using the most obvious metaphor for light there is! What about the electric bulb and light in the bathroom? What about the light in headlamps, what are they made of? She wants to google it, writes "light in headlamps" in the search field, then skims down the page and discovers that it's made from something called xenon, what about xenon, she notes it down on a piece of paper.

•

She never manages to get out of her head, does she? Oh God. She shakes her head. Shakes, shakes, shakes. She *is* just the mountains. She looks at the cursor that's blinking. She identifies with the cursor. She identifies with the cursor! Waiting, blinking, and without any real existence in the world, just on and off between blink and blink. Is *this* her light in the world?

•

A minute later, after this last thought has swelled in her head like one of those dishcloths that you can buy compressed, which don't unfold until you put them in hot water, then they swell and unfold to reveal their gaudy patterns, she phones her mother and cries, as she so often and regularly does when this happens: I only live in my head! and her mother says: no, you don't, and she says, yes, I *do*! I just sit here on this bed and look up at the mountains. And *that* in itself, that she "only lives in her head," is an unbearable cliché, and only makes everything feel even more claustrophobic. And what's more, she isn't *allowed* to think that instead of sitting here thinking, she should perhaps have spent ninety-three days in a tiny toilet stall in Rwanda with five other women hiding from the Hutus, like she saw in an episode of *60 Minutes*, because only then would she have the right to say anything real about life. It was a clichéd and claustrophobic dichotomy! She is completely one hundred percent closed off! I can't live out here with all you people. My head is my toilet. You might be exaggerating just a little, Sigrid. Yes, okay. Sorry. She'd gone too far, far too far. But I can't live out here. It's true. And at the moment I'm *not* particularly attractive either. But, Sigrid, you're so beautiful, her mother says. I am not, Sigrid retorts. Her mother laughs.

18

But, apropos of women who are mothers: was Trine at the opening of the exhibition "Women in Norwegian Art" yesterday, where she was going to do a masturbation performance? Yes. You were supposed to see her as you came in, between the bookshelves in the foyer, on a bed of small globes, semi-naked, rubbing a packet of figs bought from the supermarket against her vagina, the packet of figs was just big enough and round enough to cover her (which is to say, she was actually supposed to be wearing a pair of seamless, skin-colored cotton underwear from H&M), and she was supposed to be lying in front of a painting by Bjarne Melgaard, where he's ejaculating onto Paul Gauguin's grave. But it didn't work out that way. She couldn't do it. As she was about to get undressed in the restroom, she could feel how hard her breasts were, because she hadn't breastfed for eight hours and she normally fed Haldis every couple of hours or so. But Haldis was at home with her grandmother in Bergen right now, and Trine, who was here, had breasts that were so full of milk that they were more like a couple of absurd, rock-hard balls. It hurt, and she was annoyed that she hadn't done anything about it sooner, when she felt them getting harder, and now they were so hard that she almost couldn't squeeze them at all. She had bought a hand pump at the drugstore, because she'd planned to pump herself and keep the milk. It would be fine, she'd gotten it all worked out. But the pump was in her hotel room. And it wasn't long now until the opening. But she had to do something about her balloon tits, they might just make the whole performance seem pornographic; she didn't want it to be pornography, first of all, and second, the pressure in her tits was making her feel almost claustrophobic. Trine took a taxi back to the hotel, got the pump, hurried back to the art gallery. But when, safely ensconced in the restroom at the art gallery again, she pulled up her T-shirt and held it up by pushing her chin into her chest, undid her breastfeeding bra, took out the woolen pads, put the pump to her nipple, and pressed the handle, there was no resistance! It was as easy to press as cutting paper with well-oiled scissors. The nipple was sucked gently into the plastic tube, and she pressed and pressed and pressed the handle, but no vacuum was created, no jet of milk released. Trine sat on the toilet seat and wanted to cry. Had she really bought this manual pump for five hundred kroner and put it together wrong? Clearly! And her breasts were so sore, so tight, that they made her feel sick, made her feel that her tits were ridiculous and huge, that they might just keep on swelling and swelling into great porno boils, she *had to* get rid of this milk or she'd faint. She'd have to hand-milk. But she hated it! She'd managed to avoid any hand-milking or pumping and let her daughter empty her breasts, because for some reason she couldn't cope with seeing her own milk and pressing her own breasts and feeling the lumps of milk under her skin, but now she *had* to. She had to circle her nipple with her hand, "open like the letter C," as she remembered reading in a breastfeeding brochure, and then press in toward the breast. But her tit was so hard it actually wasn't possible to press inward! She felt the sweat pearling on her upper lip, her arms were shaking, it all made her feel so nauseous. It was a bit of a mystery, really: she had such an uncomplicated relationship with her body that she could lie on a bed made up of small globes and masturbate with a packet of figs, but to press her own breasts and squeeze out milk made her sick, sick, sick. And nothing was coming out. Was she doing it wrong? Did she have to press only the nipple, even though this was against breastfeeding law? Clearly that's what she had to do. She gingerly pressed her nipple and a tiny white drop appeared on the tip of her nipple, and then she pressed gently, stroked the sides of her breast to push the milk forward, and pressed again gently, gently. And there they came, four thin jets straight ahead into the air. Okay, she'd better take the pump off the bottle and hold it to her breast instead, then. She tried, still holding her T-shirt in place by pressing her chin into her chest, to unscrew the bottle from the pump, but her fingers were slippery from the little milk she had squeezed out and the bottle fell onto the restroom floor with a hollow plastic clunk. So the bottle was unusable, and she didn't have any other bottles with her, they were all in the hotel room. But it was ridiculous, really, that she should save the milk, her daughter would be fine with formula, why was she getting so stressed out about it? And it

really wasn't long now until she was supposed to be lying on
a bed of small globes, masturbating with a packet of figs, but
she couldn't, couldn't, could not go out there like this, the
pressure would make her faint. Fine! Trine thought, so be it:
she knelt down on the restroom floor, lifted the toilet seat, and
started to express by hand down into the toilet. The four jets
squirted here and there to begin with, but then they joined
together, and there was a funny little sound as she milked
herself, a bit like someone splitting a match, only very faint.
And then it struck her: *this* was her performance! She got her
mobile phone out of her trouser pocket, rang the curator,
and said that she'd moved her performance into the restroom,
and that the miniature globes could stay where they were in
front of the copy of Bjarne Melgaard's painting, her performance was in here. And then when she'd finished, when
she'd been watched by artist friends and an invited audience
in tight black jeans and low pumps, with scarves around
their necks and champagne glasses in their hands, and her
breasts were more or less their normal size again and felt exhausted and soft and crumpled, she sat down in the foyer,
exhausted and soft herself, and drank a glass of white wine,
with the horrible feeling that she was doing something she
shouldn't, as she hadn't had a drink since before she got pregnant. The response was good, especially from friends who
had children. Those who didn't saw a parallel with Bjarne
Melgaard's masturbation, both Trine and Melgaard produc-
ing *whiteness*, as they said. And that it was amusing how similar milking into a toilet was to throwing up after a party!
That this *combination* of two extremes, the *maternal* (breastfeeding) and the *non-maternal* (throwing up), said something

new about being a mother. She just nodded. She was so tired. And as she sat on her chair with the knowledge that hands are inferior to babies' mouths when it comes to emptying breasts, she felt she no longer belonged here. And felt that the feeling that she'd feared ever since she was pregnant was nothing to be frightened of after all. Because she was someone else now! She wanted to cry. She had clung to the idea that she would be the same person, even though she'd had a child, but she *was not* the same. Definitively not. And when she noticed that being here and doing the same sort of thing as before gave her some kind of cred, the fact that she hadn't disappeared into a hormonal haze, that she hadn't let go of her own *project*, her own *personality*, made her want to spit in their faces, rip off all her clothes, and show them the stretch marks on her belly and the stitches that had left a big lump by her ass, in fact, made her just want to lie down on the floor and *give birth* right there in front of them, and force them all to lick up the amniotic fluid and blood, then suck them all up into her body and cram them into her heart so they could hear it beating, so loudly that they'd have to cover their ears, so loudly that the rhythm pulsed into them and they all experienced being inflated for two beats before being emptied again, with the pounding of her heart. Then they would understand. She was wet with sweat, cotton-woolish, full of milk, and sitting there on the chair, with her tired arms and her crumpled, exhausted breasts after all the milking and holding them over the toilet bowl, she felt more exposed and vulnerable than she ever had before. And she almost had the feeling that she'd betrayed Haldis in some way, as she'd used her breasts, which belonged more to Haldis than her at the moment, in a performance. That she'd said something about Haldis by milking herself in the restroom. And that wasn't the point at all! She loved Haldis! She wanted to cry again. Haldis, when she was lying on her breast, her little mouth sucking and sucking, when the milk flowed, so happy, so gurglingly happy, so at ease in the world, with her. Her small, round head, her soft wisps of hair, her tiny nose pressed into Trine's breast. Haldis, oh Haldis! Had she betrayed her by doing this? She couldn't bear the thought. It felt as though she might split in two, she was so tired, as though her legs might slip out in each direction, her arms fall apart, her head fall back, that she might slide from the chair like a rag doll, legs apart, onto the floor. And then she would just lie there, as herself: a puddle of a mother. She should be at home with Haldis, she thought. But instead she's here, in this stupid hotel room, and rubbing her bare, cold feet against each other, while a pair of walruses dig for mussels on the seabed.

19

As we may remember, Linnea's legs are also bare as she stands looking out the window in Copenhagen. However, something other than the fact that they both have bare legs sticking out from a piece of clothing—an oversized man's shirt in one case and a dressing gown that was found in the hotel bathroom in the other—links Trine and Linnea, and this is that they both went to see the exhibition "Postfeminist Art" in Bergen on the same day, seventeen months ago. But they differed as far as what they liked and didn't like in the exhibition. Trine liked Tracey Emin's work, which included, among other things, her famous line drawings of drunk women in high heels, and she perhaps *particularly* liked the line drawing of a woman's crotch with a woman's hand quite clearly masturbating (on said crotch), and that under the leg it said *Oh yeh* {*sic*!} in shaky letters, as though it had been written with the other hand, haha! Trine's then inner self rejoiced. In addition, she deeply appreciated Emin's patchwork quilt with its provocative motto. She adored the fact that

Emin had used this, the oldest and most pathetic expression of female art or craftsmanship, the *quilt*, and that she'd written on them things like: "Every time I see my shit yeah I know nothing stays in my body." Linnea, on the other hand, didn't feel anything in particular at the sight of this work—that is to say, initially she felt a form of exasperated irritation; it wasn't that she couldn't appreciate what was original and daring about the presentation of provocative, naked sexual organs, she just thought they were predictable declarations that Everything Is Horrible, Everything Is Shameful, Everything Is Difficult, Broken from the Start, and Impossible to Keep Hold Of. Everything Falls to Pieces and Is Problematic. And Chaotic. Forever. Ha, ha. That, thought Linnea, was maybe true of the more depressive periods in one's life. But it's not always the case! thought Linnea, who experienced herself as the glittering but enclosed play of light in a chandelier. Linnea only found herself trembling when she stood in front of a small picture of a glittering palace, painted by Karen Kilimnik. A tiny glittering palace painted in light blue glitter on a big white surface, and a bit farther down there was a proud, rearing glitter horse, which was light blue as well, with a saddle on its back. At the bottom of the picture was the text: "Soon the glitter horse will arrive to take me to the ball at the glitter palace." And Linnea felt everything quiver, because this expressed her deepest wish in life in so many ways, it was so hopeless and childish and almost ironic, world-weary, yet *still* sincere and genuinely hopeful of finding a glitter palace and horse, and a ball. And Göran, glittering and galloping toward her, in the future. So, on that day, but at different times, two women left the exhibition, the one called Trine, who felt reinvigorated and shameless and not a little devil-may-care as she met the air outside the gallery, and the other called Linnea, who met the air full of hope as she looked up at the sky and saw that it too was light blue.

20

But here, a few days after their meeting at the Glyptotek: Linnea and Göran at the Tivoli Gardens. Göran's face with a big Ferris wheel in the background that's going around and around, and looks as though it's coming out of the left side of his head and going around to the right. And Linnea, who is standing looking at his face and the progress of the wheel into and out of his head. Göran, who is looking past Linnea because he doesn't dare look directly at her all the time for fear of forgetting his wife. Göran, who might look at Linnea and forget his own wife, and see only Linnea's beaming face. Linnea, who wishes intensely that he didn't have a wife, but who knows that he does.

•

And here: Linnea and Göran at the Tycho Brahe Museum. Linnea, standing behind Göran, who is standing studying the starry sky on the ceiling above them, and Linnea, who wishes so *intensely* that Göran didn't have a wife, but knows that he does. Göran, who just wants to let himself fall and not have a wife, and sink down into the arms of Linnea. The stars, which shine above them as though they too want something, desperately. Göran, who abruptly turns to Linnea and says, with his hand barely touching her shoulder: you, my fulgurite.

•

Here: Linnea, who doesn't understand what that means. What does that mean? Linnea asks. A fulgurite, Göran tells her, is something that is formed when lightning strikes in the desert, for example. The heat of the lightning melts the sand around the strike into a unique glass formation, a kind of root down into the sand, which is hollow in the middle, where the lightning was. I am the sand, Göran says. Oh, Linnea says, but Göran has turned away from her. She wants to put her arms around him, but can't. Linnea, who stands behind Göran and thinks: Inside him, I am glass. Inside me, I am glass. Oh, for that second, the universe is in harmony for Linnea.

•

And here: Linnea and Göran, who have completely forgotten that Göran has a wife, Lotta, as she is called, and are having sex in Göran's hotel room. Oh, the universe is in harmony for Linnea and Göran at that moment. Göran, who strokes her cheek with a finger afterward, and Linnea, who thinks with resolve that she will engrave his white hair and white beard and piercing eyes somewhere deep in her body so she never forgets. Linnea, who puts a shirt she finds in his suitcase in her bag while Göran showers.

•

And here, after Göran has left: Linnea's hand that finds a note from Göran in her trouser pocket where her hand is resting. Linnea's hand that lifts the note to Linnea's eyes, which read the note with an expression we can't quite make out, as we only see her bluish-green, glassy iris moving ever so slightly back and forth as Linnea reads the note, her eyes that suddenly remind us of fulgurites, the blueish-green, glassy iris around the pupil's channel into the eye!

21

Things are about to happen for Sigrid: she puts down the
book with a portrait of the author Kåre Tryvle on the back,
next to Dante. And then she puts on some clothes she can be
seen in, makes herself up, pulls on her green woolen coat,
which she thinks is beautiful, but hasn't found a scarf to go
with yet and so uses a green woolen scarf that in many ways
ruins the green of the coat, as the greens don't match, then
goes out the door, locks it; she just needs to walk, get out,
away. Her legs are on automatic pilot and she takes her usual
route, the one she always takes when she's in this kind of life-
crisis mood, when she thinks she just has to accept that this
is how things are. *Yes*, she will wander this earth all alone.
Yes, she just has to accept it. *Yes*, she is the only one who sees
everything she sees, and this is of no relevance to anyone else.
Everything she sees right here, right now, as she walks up
the hill toward Nordnesparken, will disappear! It won't have
made an impression on anyone other than her. And she'll
never be able to tell anyone about it, or to make it mean

something to them too. It's desperately sad, but that's the way it is. And that's how it is for you too, old man, who walks past her, looking classically old. She notices you and recognizes the tragedy of your pointless existence, which for her and everyone else who passes you is as meaningless as that of a log in water, which just floats around without knowing that it's actually floating around. Oh no, the log thought!

•

Explanation: she once saw a log, or rather, part of a trunk, floating on a lake, black and saturated by the water, and it made a deep impression on her, the fact that it was just floating like that. Blindly, unaware. In one respect, it was obvious that even a whole tree wouldn't be aware, and so even more obvious that a bit of chopped-off tree, a trunk, floating on a lake, wouldn't be aware either, neither of itself nor of where it was—that was obvious—but the sight of the log floating in the water suddenly *made something click* for Sigrid: the log has no awareness! The log doesn't know that it's waterlogged, or that it's in water. And the water doesn't know that it has a log in it. The water seeps into something but isn't aware of it. And *she* sees the log floating. *She* sees the water surround the log. Who sees *her* floating around? It gave her total claustrophobia: it was an insight, a discovery that she couldn't force her way into or out of. And now, the sight of the old man walking past her, the thought of the log makes her shudder. She never feels more claustrophobic than when she thinks about the log.

•

Or when she thinks about *das Ding an sich*—as it's also called. All knowledge about the world is mediated. We are all logs floating around in water, even if we say so ourselves.

•

Oh, *she just has to accept it*! She has to go to the lookout point with three benches and hold on to the railing that has been put up to stop people from falling over the edge, hold it tight and close her eyes as her fury at the impossibility of everything rages in her chest. She actually doesn't feel like a little human being anymore, but rather like everything that has ever been, is, and shall be. She almost laughs, because suddenly it strikes her that the words "through me you pass into eternal pain" is not about any gates to hell made of iron or stone or concrete, richly ornamented with frightening faces and open mouths, but about *the human being*, it's *the human being* one has to pass through, who is the gateway to eternity, whether it's made of pain, or happiness, or nothing. She *understands* that. Her: if we laid her down on the ground and drew around her in white chalk, we would have a flat outline of that which is *everything*. The human being. She is that outline, she makes herself think as she looks down at herself and is annoyed by the fact that she can't see herself from above, as in a film, at an angle from just above and behind her head, so that one can see the back of her head and her medium-length brown hair, her shoulders, arms hanging straight down, no, that are holding on to the iron railing, her hips, thighs that become knees, knees that become calves, calves that become ankles, ankles that become heels, heels that become feet, feet that are in shoes, soles that touch the asphalt, asphalt that covers the soil, soil that changes into clay, clay that reaches down to the core of the earth, the core of the earth that is magma, which regularly spews out of craters in the form of lava here and there on the surface, or is pumped up through cracks in the seabed, where it forms into what is called pillow lava, which looks a bit like a pile of books when it hardens. From this perspective, a dizzying perspective, really, the camera just above and behind her head, we can look down on the apartment buildings far below, on the fjord, the great cranes on the other side of the fjord, and Laksevåg. Heaven and a kind of ocean. The music for this scene: heroic.

•

But this all started with *her* outline, before the heroic perspective took over. Her: yes, no point in going over it all again. Brain cells, blood vessels, teeth, etc. Quite simply, a body. But contained in that body is a fury, and suddenly, an insight: the insight that, *even though* it will disappear, this outline that isn't seen from above and behind her head but from the inside, from *her* perspective, from where she can't see the back of her own head or her own face but only her hands holding on to the railing, and the red paint that's flaking off the metal, and everything else in front of her, the light, the trees—the feeling of seeing all this, and the feeling that it means something, something incredibly important, is not felt in vain, even though she can't tell anyone about it, even though she won't be able to get it to mean something in someone else's life. Because *she* sees it. Sigrid looks at her hands. They are bent around the flaking metal railing. She wants to kiss them. She bends down toward her hands and is about to kiss them when she notices that two other hands have joined hers on the railing, farther away, and she has to think of something logical to do with her mouth that is now two inches away from her knuckles. And what she decides to do is rub her chin against them, as though she were scratching her chin, as though that's what you do when your hands are stuck on a railing and you have to scratch your chin. You bend down and rub your chin against your knuckles while still indicating, by the manner in which you so naturally rub your chin against your knuckles, that you know very well it's a strange thing to do, but it's just that it seemed a natural thing to do there and then, as when you're out skiing and stand leaning against your ski poles, and if your chin itches, you bring your chin to your hands, rather than vice versa, since your hands are busy holding your ski poles. But Sigrid barely has time to think all this before a man's voice says: nice day for rubbing your chin against your knuckles, and Sigrid looks up from where she has her chin on her knuckles. She blushes when she sees the owner of the hands on the railing: it's him. It's Kåre Tryvle! The man in the portrait of the author that she's stared at for hours and laid her cheek against and longed to be turned around and taken into his arms in the way that Charlotte is taken into the arms of Bob Harris in the last scene of *Lost in Translation*, he's standing there with his hands on the same railing as hers, the railing that's there to prevent people from falling over the edge.

22

But what was written on the note that Linnea found in her trouser pocket after Göran had left? Strangely enough, not a fitting quote from some ancient Greek poem, but a poem by the American writer Richard Brautigan, which we will not include in order to avoid permission issues (but which can otherwise be found in the not-so-critically-acclaimed [yet beautiful] collection *June 30th, June 30th*, about Brautigan's lonely trip to Japan), where he, in this poem we won't quote in its entirety, compares dreams to wind: "Dreams are like the [the] / wind. They blow by."

•

The obvious reason for Göran giving her this poem is that he wanted to say that they were like the dreams, which blow by, like the breezes and wind. Like air in movement. And it wasn't until much later that Linnea discovered that the strange thing about this poem, namely the double "the [the] wind," could in one sense also mean hands in the air, because "*te*" is the Japanese word for hand, hands, and if you think, as Linnea did, that *h* is the human sound that most closely resembles air in movement (try saying hhhhhhhhhhhh), and then add the sound *h* to the word *"te,"* you get the English word "the," here used to make "wind" definite. Thus, thought Linnea, the two words "hands" and "wind" met and became one word: "the." Linnea had to hold the note to her bosom when she discovered this, because that was what was so terrible and so lovely: that they were like hands of air reaching out to each other, but unable to get a hold. And that was what made their meeting so beautiful, the air hands reaching out from their bodies, that when they stood next to each other, there were air hands touching the other, air hands stroking the other's hair, air hands around the other as they walked side by side, and when they parted: that they were air hands reaching out to each other.

•

And *that* feeling was what Linnea wanted to capture in her film!

23

But Robert, who is holding open a taxi door for Linnea right now, doesn't know all that and he feels the drag of air around her as she passes him and sits down in the taxi, a faint scent of mild soap or shampoo. He gets in and says, the Glyptotek, to the taxi driver. The Glyptotek, the taxi driver repeats slowly, what's the address? It surprises Robert that a taxi driver in Copenhagen doesn't know the Glyptotek. Um, let me see, he says, and looks in his briefcase for a tourist brochure. Dantes Plads 7, Robert says. Hmm? says the taxi driver, and Robert shows him the address in the brochure. Okay, says the taxi driver, and starts the car. New, the taxi driver explains, pointing to himself. Aha, Robert says. Where are you from? he asks. Japan, the taxi driver says. Aha, Robert replies.

•

Then no one says anything for a while. Linnea sits and looks out the window. He feels his heart hammering. It's getting closer, the time when he has to say what he's got to say. How to start? Maybe he could start with another subject? Japan! It hits him. That's the perfect starting point. Did you know, he says to Linnea as they drive through the streets of Copenhagen, that four tectonic plates meet in Japan? And that's why there are so many earthquakes there. There's a lot of tension between the plates, they don't fit seamlessly together but kind of butt into each other, so there's a buildup of pressure, and when this gets too much, it's released and triggers an earthquake. Hmm, says Linnea. Naturally, she doesn't realize that Robert has thought of using this earthquake metaphor about his own feelings, about his inner tremors and the problem with the film. Like hope, Robert thinks, and reality, which grind against each other. He's glad to have found such a fantastic metaphor, he who's normally no good with metaphors. Is that not true, he asks the driver, leaning forward, that Japan is on top of four plates . . . and the driver smiles but obviously hasn't understood, that Japan, Robert says, and identifies Japan as a point up in the air, and then indicates below this point, on top of, Robert continues, and at the bottom point, he flattens his hands out and tries to simulate tectonic plates meeting, moves his hands back and forth, aaa, says the driver, kung fu! Yes, kung fu, yes, the driver says. Chinese, he says.

24

The funeral reception back in 1998 is over, and Viggo is standing watching his relatives leave the chapel basement like a little black stream. Not, he thinks, to run out into the black sea of sorrow, but to put their everyday clothes back on and continue doing whatever it was they were doing before they got dressed in black, dreading the grief of the chapel, to reminisce and cry. The fishmonger's daughter says goodbye to him on her way out, with a little hesitation, she doesn't know whether she should stop or not, so she stops when she's almost past him, almost, he thinks, like syncopation, like a note that's held longer, an arc between stopping and walking. And in the middle of the syncopation's two legs: a little fishmonger's daughter with flat, flyaway hair and a reticent expression. He forgot to ask her name! What's your name? he childishly calls after her. Elida, she replies, and waves. Elida.

•

He stands there until everyone has left and then looks at the room around him: the green curtains that are blowing ever so slightly because someone has forgotten to close a window, the sad, square wooden ceiling lights and the linoleum floor, gray and worn. And the tables: cold. And the chairs: naked, tired, brown, and hard, with thin legs that look like steel bones. And he thinks: Is this really where I loved being as a child? Running around between the tables, hiding from Grandma behind the pillars? Sitting on her lap and eating waffles, buying raffle tickets when there was a bazaar? Drawing the raffle tickets and maybe winning a set of bathroom scales or a pair of knitting needles? Yes. And look at the room now! So Grandmaless, so lacking a bazaar, and so of itself. This is how it looked before as well, when I wasn't here. And the room has stood like this, unchanged, for all these years and allowed people to come in and out, it's just stood here and stood here, and one day I walked out and didn't know that I wouldn't come back before today, and one day Gran walked out and didn't know that she would never come back, and none of us knew that it was here we would meet again, at this meeting that isn't a meeting. This is what the room looks like when there's no one in it. And that's what it looked like back then, only I couldn't see it. I only saw Grandma, the other grandmothers, raffle tickets and prizes. Viggo suddenly sees the orange bucket standing in the corner of the room, full of flowers, the orange bucket that she used to keep her gardening tools in, they've taken it here with them and gathered up all the bouquets. He stares and stares at the bucket. Orange, full of flowers. It won't explode, he says quietly to himself. He feels a lump in his throat. He wants to cry.

•

Being here, where he hasn't been since he was a child and came to the bazaar with his grandma, brings everything back again, and he sees himself and Ståle playing by the river near the churchyard, three minutes' walk from school, Ståle, whom he was put beside in primary school to calm him down, as he was a quiet and clever boy. The positive consequences of this pairing were obvious: the noisiest pupil in the class learned a poem by heart and recited it with panache at the Christmas show at the end of the first year that Viggo and Ståle sat beside each other. A touching memory for Viggo, he has to admit, when he remembers how he and Ståle sat in the small storeroom at school where they kept all the puppets and costumes and flags and banners and musical instruments, which seemed to hang in such a way that he now recalls them as nearly falling off the walls on top of them, even though it obviously wasn't like that, but it must have just seemed like it because he remembers it from below, from a height of about 4.43 feet, if he's going to be precise. And how he read line after line of the poem and Ståle repeated and repeated it, and he directed him: "More feeling there, take a pause there," and how he encouraged him and said things like "You're *so* good!" when Ståle remembered a verse and recited it with conviction and all the right pauses, and how Ståle seemed to rise up onto his toes when he said something with a lot of feeling. And how finally Ståle lit up when he managed the whole thing by heart, and how he recited it at the Christmas show, so confident, with conviction and all the right pauses, and rising up on his toes, and how he himself, Viggo, sitting in the audience, felt when the applause erupted that he had done something good in this life. Viggo's eyes filled with tears. But back to the list of consequences of putting a noisy pupil alongside a quiet pupil: the first consequence was (a) that the noisy pupil learned poems by heart, and this was the consequence that the teachers saw. But they didn't see consequence (b) that the noisy pupil paid the quiet pupil to do his math homework, or consequence (c) that despite this mercantile relationship, a genuine friendship developed between the quiet and the noisy pupil, which meant that the noisy pupil always defended the quiet pupil, both verbally and physically, when other pupils (ranging from the merely noisy to the uncontrollable to the complete idiots) threw fir cones or stones at the quiet pupil when he sat in the bicycle shed reading books while the others played football. Or consequence (d) a slight doubt in the quiet pupil that the friendship was really real, and not just bought and paid for, or consequence (e) that this slight doubt would vanish when he many years later met Ståle again by accident, at Universitetsplassen, and Ståle was in charge of the business school's annual show and got drugs for his fellow students and looked after Viggo. Nor did the teachers see consequence (f) that Viggo drank and partied and drifted and drank for three weeks, until in the end there came the sad consequence (g) that the quiet pupil had completely left himself behind.

•

Viggo thinks, as he sits by the orange bucket and the tears have stopped rolling down his cheeks, that he just has to *cut through everything and take action*, he has to do something with the situation now, that is to say, his life: he needs to be himself again. He must, suddenly it's very clear to him, become himself again! He feels the urge to stand up, hold out his arms, and stand there with his arms up, and let the perspective rotate around him, up and up through the air, until one sees him only as a tiny person standing on the surface of the earth with his arms outstretched, embracing everything: the world and his own fate as a reader, as a dreamer, as a thinker, and not as a party animal, and, because the perspective is rotating up and up from a tiny man with outstretched arms in a chapel basement, we're filled with a strange sensation of centrifugal force: total encapsulation and expansion, and extreme concentration, around a single point. Which is Viggo. And inside Viggo: Viggo's heart. But the rotating perspective reaches no farther than the chapel roof, where it has to give up with a dull thud. And Viggo drops his arms again, feels just as tremulous as before.

25

It's incredible, but by the railing that's been put up to stop people from falling over the edge, this happens: Kåre Tryvle takes one of his hands from the railing, holds it out, and says "Kåre" and Sigrid then releases one of her hands, takes Kåre's, and says "Sigrid." Kåre means "the one with the curly hair," did you know that? Sigrid says. Yes, I did know that once upon a time, but I realize I haven't thought about it for a while, Kåre says. They smile at each other, look out over the water at Laksevåg, then back at each other. There is silence, until Sigrid says: I read it in a book of names once, when I was wondering what my potential future children should be called. And at the back of the book, the man who'd gathered all the names uses Kåre as an example of a name with a specific meaning that you should perhaps be wary of, as you can't be sure that your child will have curls. And you don't exactly have a lot of curls, so it looks like your parents made a mistake.

•

The fact that she's saying all this is incredible, it's a lie, since she looked up Kåre in the name book specifically to find out what it means, and in the hope that it would mean "protection" or "home." Kåre laughs. No, that's right, I don't have a lot of curls. And what does Sigrid mean? he asks. Oh, it's got a fantastic meaning, she says, and surprises herself by talking so eagerly, yet charmingly, about the meaning of names, to this man whose cheek she stroked in a miniature portrait in black and white: I'm really happy with it and use every opportunity to tell people; it means both "victory" and "beautiful woman." So, paradoxically, I ought to be well-prepared for dealing with life, she says. Paradoxically, you say, Kåre says, so you don't deal with life very well? No, I wouldn't say that, Sigrid says, and they laugh, in the way one laughs when one laughs at something just to laugh at it, because it's been presented in such a way that you're required to laugh, even though it isn't particularly funny, something of which the person who said it must be well aware. If one didn't laugh, it would be embarrassing for the person who said it. On the whole, statements like this can serve as a kind of watershed in communication between two speakers, whether they're on the same wavelength or not. Even though the person who said it realizes that it wasn't the best thing to say, and would rather not have said it at all, because by making this mild complaint one has forced the other party down to one's own level with sympathetic laughter, a laughter that's not about the situation itself, but what was "funny" about the sentence, which wasn't funny at all. But Sigrid and Kåre are on the same wavelength, they can feel it already as they stand there with their hands on the railing. Kåre even liked the fact that she

didn't deal with life particularly well, she could see that, he
liked that. "The question is, what's holding you back?" Kåre
says in a clear, resonant, quotey voice. He straightens himself
up, then says in a serious, exaggeratedly deep voice, "There
are a few things you don't know and they are what are holding you back." He takes a pause. "*What* is it that you don't
know?" he asks, with particular emphasis on "what." "A few
basic principles, that's all. Principles are those ideas that are
the same for everyone, they never change over time and they
create the positive effects you want." He pauses again. Sigrid
looks at him and gives him a shrewd smile, because she's not
sure where he's going with this, so a shrewd smile seems like
the best response. "Once you *understand* and *accept* these few
principles, your golf swing and your golf game will improve.
And your improvement will be permanent." Sigrid laughs.
I'll remember that, she says. Life is golf, don't ever forget,
Kåre says. He pulls a book out of his bag and says, as he
holds the book out to her, you simply have to read this book,
it's called *Golf Can't Be This Simple*. She takes the book, and
they laugh at the title. They look out over Laksevåg, and
Sigrid isn't quite sure what to do with the golf book, she
flicks through it and says, yes, I definitely need to get this.
They look out over Laksevåg. The cranes on the other side are
no longer in use, and the open dry docks lie there gaping in
the water. The hillsides behind are covered in spruce trees.
To the left there's a peak that's higher than the others, and
one of the slopes is smooth and treeless, and probably sweeps
down to a lake behind the mountain that stands in front,
hiding it.

•

There's a pause in the conversation, when both wonder what
they should say next, and Sigrid has time to feel in the pit of
her stomach that she's standing next to Kåre Tryvle, and
Kåre Tryvle has the time to glance over at Sigrid and think
that she's sweet.

•

It's a bit of a drag that my name only means "curlylocks," to
be honest, Kåre says after the pause, I would much rather
it meant "beautiful woman," or at least "victory." Yes, I can
understand that, it *is* good for one's name to mean something
like that, then at least you've got *that* to pull out of your hat,
Sigrid says, relieved that the conversation is flowing again,
but she realizes that everything she's said so far has given
away the fact that her life isn't great, even though she's said it
in a way that makes him laugh, and even though it seems as
though one might be more sympathetic to people who don't
deal too well with life rather than people who do, she doesn't
want to complain, so she says: but things aren't so bad, the
flat-share I live in even has a washing machine. And if I get
the golf book, I should get it all sorted out in no time. My
improvement *will* be permanent! Kåre laughs. I have to admit that I think I know who you are, she blurts out, and feels
a kind of nervous pull. Oh, he says. Yes, I think you're the
one who wrote a book called *An Empty Chair*, aren't you? Sigrid blushes and puts her hands to her cheeks, now I'm blushing, she says, might as well just admit it, even though it
probably doesn't really *help* to hide your cheeks when you're
blushing! You look like the photo of the author and have
the same name as the man who wrote the book, so from that
I've kind of deduced that you must be the same man—this
man called Kåre who's standing here, without any curls—

but I didn't know if I should mention it. Kåre puts his hands to his cheeks and says: I'm not blushing, but that's not because I never blush, because now I'm blushing a little inside. I hope you thought the book was okay. Sigrid looks at the ground, because this is an impossible topic, she who's put her cheek to his portrait! "Okay," Sigrid says, is a very small word for what it was, I was completely overwhelmed by what you wrote. It was like something you're always waiting for but don't know if it's ever going to happen. For someone to *see* what you're thinking, understand it. Your *vision* . . . the way you've composed it, the way it . . . (she can't say what she's thinking about *the empty chair*, that she's somehow been waiting to find it waiting for her, in real life) . . . Kåre smiles sheepishly, he's longed for someone to say something like this about his vision and the way he's expressed it, for them to see what he sees, and to see that what he sees is good, that he sees clearly and deeply, and he's embarrassed that he couldn't manage to smile less sheepishly, he focuses on a plane that's flying over them, that contains, he thinks, if it's a normal SAS Braathens plane, about a hundred passengers he knows nothing about, who, at the same second that he's standing down here and looking up and smiling sheepishly, are doing things he knows nothing about, but can imagine: scratching their heads, reading the in-flight magazine, drinking coffee, and definitely, definitely: sitting . . . How it . . . Sigrid says, and lets out an awkward laugh, how it, by using *good old-fashioned storytelling* . . .

•

There now follows a longish passage that describes how Sigrid tries to put into words why Kåre's book is so wonderful and insightful, which has a lot to do with "how good old-fashioned storytelling in the form of poetry in many ways is an *immanent testimony* to the desire for cohesion, the desire to hold things together" and how the picture of an empty chair is a humble demonstration of this desire, I mean, *putting out a chair for someone*, Sigrid says as she gesticulates carefully in the air with her hands, and then we'll hear how Kåre tries to formulate what's so wonderful and insightful about what Sigrid has said about his book (saying that no one's ever said anything like that to him, that no one's ever gotten to the heart of what he's writing like this before, that she has a special eye—Sigrid is *so* happy! She has longed for this, that someone would see what she sees, and see that what she sees is good, will say that she has a *special eye*, and she too smiles sheepishly and feels embarrassed that she can't smile any less sheepishly; she focuses on another plane flying over them, that contains, she thinks, if it's a normal SAS Braathens plane, about a hundred passengers she knows nothing about, who, at the same second that she's standing down here and looking up and smiling sheepishly, are doing things she knows nothing about, but can imagine: scratching their heads, reading the in-flight magazine, drinking coffee, and definitely, definitely: sitting), how he looks a bit embarrassed when he says it, embarrassed because he's attracted attention to himself by saying something about how she's shown *him* attention, and then about how Sigrid takes this: how she understands it and tries to help him out by elaborating on what she's said, and how her eyes are completely naked when she says it, so he'll understand that she really means it, that his book *has* touched something in her heart. And because her eyes are so naked when she says this,

his eyes become totally naked when he accepts the compliment, and this gives rise to one of those moments so rarely shared between two people: when both have naked eyes. They can both feel it, and are both astonished and unsettled by the feeling, a kind of secret lightning bolt of emotion deep inside them both, and so they look away from each other and the rare moment seems to come to an end, but it has taken root in them. They exchange some more compliments, they glance secretly at each other, and they are very, very beautiful in this slightly ridiculous, but all the same genuine, situation of new beginnings and understanding and perhaps, *perhaps* love? Another plane flies in from the left-hand side of the sky and Sigrid is glad to have something else to look at, she feels warm and strange, she would love to stand here forever, but it's almost too exhausting. Nice plane, Kåre says, and Sigrid laughs and nods. It's strange, isn't it, Kåre says, that up there in the plane there are probably about a hundred people doing things we know nothing about, but can imagine, scratching their heads, reading the in-flight magazine, drinking coffee, and they all have their individual lives, but we can only see them as a narrow plane in the sky? Sigrid nods, it's so strange, she says, I know exactly what you mean, I think about things like that too! And right then, a big van reverses up the hill that leads out to the main road behind where they're standing, just as a small car turns down the same slope, and neither of the vehicles has seen the other, and there's a bump as these two movements, "reversing up" and "turning down," collide, and Sigrid and Kåre turn, and Sigrid says: Oops!

II

MIDDAYS

1

Sigrid and Kåre walk toward the crash, but then two ladies in white coats come dashing out from a building to the right. It's an old people's home, or a nursing home, Sigrid says to Kåre. The young driver of the big van is standing by the door of the small car; he turns toward the ladies in white coats who come running, and when they get to the crash, these running white coats, an old lady with white hair gets out of the small car and shoos them off with angry hands, as though they were cows standing in the way. Looks like they can manage without us, Kåre says. Shall we go back down into town? Sigrid nods.

•

Sigrid and Kåre walk side by side down toward the city center, and neither of them says anything. Sigrid holds her shoulder bag with both hands, Kåre has his hands in his pockets. He looks up at the cars as they drive past, and he's not particularly happy: the state of things has caught up with him again (perhaps partly because of the crash), and now he's *ambivalent*, it's so typical, he thinks. That right now, when he was going to have a whole month to himself, clean and unspoiled, because he's just broken up with Wanda, right now, just when he was going to have all this time to meditate and to sort things out in peace and quiet—who he *was*, what he *wanted* in life, what *mistakes* he'd made, if even the ultimate woman was wrong for him, what he was going to do now— that right now, of all moments, a young girl who spoke like an oracle should be standing next to him at the top of a hill. As if his life weren't hard enough already, that he should feel the urge to get to know her better. He almost felt that it was *she* who could tell him who he was and what he should do. And all that after nothing more than a conversation by a railing. Not even Wanda had said things like that, Wanda, who was the one he'd put the chair out for. Ah well, no matter what, Kåre thinks as he walks beside Sigrid without saying a word, he isn't going to mess up his clean month, during which he is going to meditate and find peace with the help of vegetables, exercise, books, and films, because of some unexpected feeling that this girl *warmed* him, somehow. That she, in some magical way, acknowledged him, acknowledged who he was. He looks up at nothing in particular. And yet wasn't it, he thinks—ambivalent again—terrifically symbolic that there should be a crash right behind them, and that it was a *young* driver who crashed into an *old* driver, a good deal older than himself, to be fair, but all the same. As though he weren't an open wound already, he thinks, with bitter self-irony, that he should feel the universe was laughing at him as he stood there, an old man, together with the young Sigrid, and all his thoughts of a clean month and vegetables falling away because of one deep and enthralling look. He *hasn't* changed a bit, Kåre concludes, in this tangle of self-reflection that he's struggling through as he walks down toward the city center.

•

As she walks the only thing Sigrid feels is that she's not present in her own body, that her arms, as both are holding on to her bag, feel strangely linked to each other in a kind of unbreakable circle, and that this circle is growing and growing until it's the only thing she can feel, physically, in this world, as though her arms were an unbroken ring, and as though the rest of her body were falling away, trailing behind, numb. It's quite probable that she feels like this because she's clinging on to her bag for dear life, she feels it acutely, that she's tensing her hands, tensing the muscles that hold and pull at her bag, and she tries to relax, loosen her hold, which makes her legs feel oddly light, but more present. She finds the whole situation so awkward, walking beside Kåre, whose author portrait she's stroked. She wants to tell him that the avenue they're walking down is incredibly beautiful in summer, when it's full of green leaves that weave together overhead as you walk, as though you were walking through a green tunnel or something, but then she suddenly thinks it's a silly thing to say, it would be better to say that it's beautiful now, in January, when all the pruned branches are visible with all their knots and look like they're shaking their bare fists at the sky, but then she thinks that's silly as well, and definitely a bit too poetic, and soon they'll reach the end of the avenue anyway. Why can't she just be like she was back there? Sigrid thinks and looks at the old wooden houses that line the road, behind the trees, why does she suddenly have to deliberate and weigh up every word, why can't she just say things straight-out, is it impossible to achieve such an unthought-through but freely speaking state now that she's thought about it? It's incredibly beautiful here in summer, says Sigrid, who's determined to conquer herself, trying to catch herself off guard, feeling that she's blushing again. Really? he says. Yes, it's extremely green, Sigrid says. Hmm, Kåre replies. And then there's silence again. They walk like this until they come to a café, and Kåre asks, despite all his thoughts about the flashing and highly symbolic warning lights set off by the car crash, if maybe they should go in and have a coffee.

2

But Kåre says to the waitress that he'd like a glass of red
wine, and the soup of the day, what is it? Onion. Sigrid's face
tries to hide the fact that she's thinking "but it's only eleven
o'clock in the morning!" and that she's unsure what to do
now, if she should order a glass of wine too—and she's only
got a few seconds to decide!—so that she doesn't seem boring
and to show that having a glass of wine at midday, or even in
the morning, is hardly unthinkable for her, but then, on the
other hand: if she orders wine, it might look like she's just
doing the same as him, which would make her seem depen-
dent and subservient, and maybe it's more important to do
the opposite of what he does, and in any case: drinking wine
in the morning *is* totally unthinkable for her, because then,
after drinking wine in the morning, she would never be able
to get any of the other things she has to do today done; after
drinking wine she might as well give up trying to write any
more of her article. But then again, maybe it's time to get out
of her head and to let go of the tight reins she always keeps

on herself, isn't it about time she did *in fact* order a glass of wine at eleven o'clock and forget about the article? Even though she's *actually* quite disappointed that he's ordered wine, when he asked if she wanted to go in for a *coffee*? Every fiber in her body seems to be telling her *this just isn't going to work, whatever this is*, because she's *not* the sort to drink wine in the morning, and she can't really marry someone who drinks wine in the morning either. But then, maybe, if their love was strong enough? And what about the onion soup? She looks at the menu and sees that it costs 135 kroner, and she can't afford that, and in any case, onions aren't good for her stomach. I think I'll just have a cup of tea, she says, with milk, please. Or actually, what teas do you have? (She might not need milk if they don't have anything other than fruit or herb tea.) We've got fruit teas, herb teas, or Earl Grey, the waitress says. Sigrid normally only drinks black tea. Fruit tea isn't really tea, and herb teas generally taste like grass. I'll take an Earl Grey, she says. Are you sure you don't want a glass of wine? Kåre asks, come on, it's so boring, drinking alone. He laughs. She blushes. She has to be firm, she has to show that she's independent. No, I think I'll stick to tea, I have to finish writing an article later on. The waitress nods, with a kind of ironic expression on her face. Sigrid can hear how the words "I'll stick to" made a stiff white lace collar sprout from her blouse. She blushes so hard that she has to bend over to check that her shoelaces are tied properly, so it might possibly look like her face is only red because the blood rushed to her head when she bent down. But she doesn't have shoelaces, she's got her boots on, hasn't she? It will just have to be a mystery, the fact that she bends down, she has her

reasons for doing it! She puts a hand to her forehead. I'm
hot, she says. You're stressed, Kåre says, and takes her hand.
Don't worry, he says. She looks at him. Can he really see that,
that she's stressed? Does he really understand? No one's ever
said that to her before! She tries to lower her shoulders. Okay,
she says, and smiles.

•

Kåre's and Sigrid's hands are clasped in the middle of the
table. Several seconds have passed; they still haven't let go.
His hands are clasping hers, such that his thumbs fold her
hands in. The underside of his hands touch her hands, the
skin on the upper part of her hands touches the skin on
the underside of his. We should point out that this contact
makes a cock tighten on one side of the table, and some nipples harden on the other side of the table. The surface of the
table under their hands gets moist, but the rest of the table
remains cold.

•

No one sees this. There's only a couple of old ladies sitting
beyond the big glass wall behind Kåre's back, on the mez-
zanine below. The five big blue vases standing along the
one wall are full of branches, which are full of small white
flowers—fake. The waitress passes the vases as she comes
up the stairs carrying a tray with the drinks on it, and is
the only one who catches Sigrid and Kåre holding hands,
and they immediately let go when they see the waitress
coming, and they both look down at the table, so they don't
see that the waitress is thinking something along the lines
of: aha!

•

Could I have a glass of wine after all? Sigrid asks. But white, not red? For some reason, red wine gives her a sore tummy. *Of course* you can, the waitress says, and Sigrid doesn't like the look deep in the waitress's eyes, as though she's saying, you caved in, you chicken, weren't you going to *stick* to tea? and she doesn't like the waitress's attitude, so she says: Could you make it two glasses, while you're at it? Two glasses of white wine? the waitress asks. Yes, two glasses, Sigrid says, and feels like laughing, just to unsettle the waitress, as revenge because, deep in her eyes, she called her a chicken. By ordering something as unheard-of as two glasses of white wine at once, with such a shameless expression on her face, she's got her own back. She can see that the waitress just thinks: idiot, but for her, it was worth it, that small moment when the woman was taken aback. Sigrid looks at Kåre now and does burst out laughing because he too looks taken aback. As though she *has* done something entirely unheard-of. No point in being stingy, Sigrid says, and she has to admit that she rather likes the fact that he looks a bit embarrassed when the waitress comes back with two glistening glasses of white wine that she puts on the table, one next to the other, perfectly positioned next to the steaming cup of tea, there, says the waitress. Lovely, says Sigrid, perfect, thank you very much! And could I have some onion soup as well? Some onion soup, not a problem, the waitress says. It's almost as though Kåre is shrinking on his seat, because she's done the unthinkable and ordered two glasses of white wine at once, in this posh café with its blue and purple and brown interior, and onion soup at 135 kroner a bowl. Now, what shall I have first? Sigrid says, and has no idea where this cavalier attitude has come from, shall I have a sip of tea, or of the first glass of wine or the second? Kåre laughs, still surprised. You win the prize for the strangest order in a café, he says, and hands her an air trophy, which she accepts, then lifts up over her head and says: I'll start with the white wine that's farthest away. And then she takes a sip of the white wine that is standing nearest the edge of the table, and puts the glass back down exactly where it stood.

3

Robert feels powerless as he sits in the taxi and Linnea keeps looking out the window. Everything was ruined when the taxi driver thought he meant "kung fu," when he was actually going to use Japan, scene of so many terrible earthquakes, as a symbolic comparison and the means to introduce his own two earthquakes: that her film is not going to be made, and the hopefully more positive earthquake: that he's in love with her. But now the mood is light and silly, Robert leans in toward the window and feels helpless. He thinks about the horse head he read about on the *Bergens Tidende* website earlier on. It turned out it was the Bergen Aquarium that had thrown it away, and there was a perfectly reasonable explanation as to why they had a horse head, even if it had ended up in the wrong dump; they'd been demonstrating an old eel fishing method that involved sinking a horse head into the water, it attracted the eels, which ate the coat and hide and flesh and then got stuck inside, so then all one had to do was pull up a horse head full of eels. A bit like

Medusa's hair! Robert thinks there's something horrible about the thought of a severed horse head sinking down through the water, he can picture it sinking down and down, with the same frozen expression on its face, down and down through the water, a horse head with no majestic horse body attached, just water where the great body should be, the muzzle forced open by the water, or perhaps frozen by rigor mortis. He doesn't know for sure, but he thinks about the eels that are stuck in the head and how when the head is pulled up through the water, the revolting gray eels must twist and turn out of it. And he thinks about the picture of the horse head that was taken underwater, where the black hide and flesh had been gnawed away, and the horse head shone white and pink and was somehow blurred, as though in a mist, teeth joined in a grimace—there was something distant about it, and lost. There it lay, the head, revealing its innards, with the same horsey grin that horses always have. The fundamental principle of all horses. Robert has to look over at Linnea. She's sitting with her face turned away and suddenly she looks so grotesque, the skin over her cheekbones, her nasal bones, the lips over her teeth, the principle for all of Linnea, deep in her own thoughts.

•

Ugh, this *won't* do! He's unable to open his mouth to speak. And then he manages it, he opens his mouth, but: no. I saw a horse head, Robert starts, but Linnea doesn't turn around, she doesn't even notice.

4

Kåre tries not to be one of those snobs who'd let themselves
be embarrassed by such a transgression of café etiquette, but
he is a bit embarrassed, he really is, he wishes she could just
finish one glass so that her two glasses would look more normal: an empty one that's been drunk standing next to a full
one that's just been ordered. Even though there's no one there
to see, that's what he wishes. To break free from the twofold
embarrassment of a lapse in etiquette and of being an old snob,
Kåre says: I've actually just been given a trophy. Real gold?
Sigrid asks. Very real, Kåre says. I won a golf tournament, in
fact, Kåre says, believe it or not, I won a tournament that four
of my best friends and I took part in. It was a glorious experience. Do you really play golf? Sigrid asks. Yes, I play golf.
Did you know that golf is the fastest-growing sport in Norway, and that there's a total of one hundred and eighteen
thousand members in the Norwegian Golf Federation? One
hundred and *eighteen* thousand? Sigrid says. One hundred
and eighteen thousand, Kåre says. They laugh. Golf is a sport

I know nothing about, it's never really grabbed me, Sigrid says. To be honest, I have to admit it seems pretty boring, a sport for businessmen and American presidents. Kåre looks at her in surprise. You know what, he starts. But then he stops. Do I know what what? Sigrid asks. Naaaah, Kåre draws it out, I never really tell people what I'm writing about, because if I do, it seems to evaporate, but what you said just now was . . . He sits staring straight ahead, with a pensive look on his face, evaluating whether he should tell Sigrid about what he's writing or not. He wants to. He wants to! he says, but he doesn't know whether it's a good idea (though he feels that it's okay to tell Sigrid, because she'll understand) . . . I'd love to know, Sigrid says. Okay, Kåre says, he's made up his mind. The thing is that . . . (how can he tell her about the article in *Vanity Fair*, the magazine that Wanda used to buy, when she was his girlfriend, something she had ceased to be exactly one week ago today, the article that was the starting point for his latest project, how can he tell Sigrid about all that without including Wanda in the telling, and without thinking too much about Wanda, who, right now, by the way, is freshly showered and smoking a cigarette out of her teenage bedroom window, with PJ Harvey on her headphones, singing, still feeling desperate inside: "I'm scared baby! I wanna run! This world's crazy! Give me the gun!" with tears welling up in her eyes, and so Kåre decides to say that he bought the magazine specifically because of the article, which was advertised on the front cover, but then, to be funny, he'll say he's lying, because of course he only buys *Vanity Fair* in order to find out how to get fuller lips) . . .

5

The thing is, Kåre says, he's going to write a novel in which
George W. Bush will be one of the main characters. It's
based on a photograph of Bush Senior and Junior on a golf
course that he found in *Vanity Fair*, in which the father has a
comforting hand on the son's shoulder. They're both wearing black golfing caps and stripy golf shirts, and Bush Junior's mouth is a narrow line, pulling toward one cheek, as
though he's thinking *damn*, and the expression in his eyes is
one of exasperation. He has, Kåre says, that man, one of the
most expressive faces in international politics, I'll give him
that. Kåre imitates the facial expression. Sigrid laughs.
Sigrid likes this, she likes the way he's interpreted this picture, she feels it cascade through her, she likes it! And the
text underneath explains it all, Kåre says, it says "Father
and son at the Cape Arundel Golf Club, in Kennebunkport,
on the son's 55th birthday, July 6, 2001. The handshake
follows George W.'s missed putt on the 18th hole." Kåre
laughs, having quoted the caption, a complicit laugh that

Sigrid feels embarrassed that she can't quite emulate; she tries, only doesn't quite manage it, though she does think that in *isolation*, at least, it's amusing, that he missed a putt on the eighteenth hole, but if there's some big political allusion here then it's passed her by, and she hopes her laughter caused by the eighteenth hole and the word "putt" covers it! She's impressed, she says, that Kåre can remember the whole caption, and Kåre smiles, he likes things like that, remembering things like that and saying them in an American movie-trailer voice. He thinks it adds a little something extra to whatever he's talking about, the fact that he can quote word-for-word from memory gives his subject extra weight, he doesn't just sit there and mumble "Eh, what did it say again, something about . . ." thus making the quote (which doesn't actually need to be a quote, but could equally well be a description of a situation) sound clumsy and flat and boring to listen to. Better by far, when you come across things like that, to learn whatever it is by heart, so you can quote it with authority on a suitable occasion. And suitable occasions always popped up, no need to worry about that. But, naturally, he doesn't say any of this, he just says, in his deep, American movie-trailer voice: "Memory, that warder of the brain," and explains that he has to remember things like that to avoid going senile. He's an old man, you see. You're not that old, Sigrid says, and looks at the table, because she shouldn't really have even remotely implied that he might be anywhere near "old," so she saves the situation by saying—I mean: seventy-four, you're still young! Kåre laughs. He looks at her. Forty-three, he says, as though it's a warning. I'm forty-three.

Twenty-three, Sigrid says. I'm twenty-three. Their ages meet in the air, perhaps largely due to the perfect symmetry in the numbers forty-three and twenty-three, but for other reasons as well, as though they were bodies and not numbers. And they too tremble.

6

And speaking of trembling, here's Viggo, still standing in the chapel basement in 1998, trembling beside the orange bucket. Dear Viggo. Do you know what we wish for you? For you to learn kung fu. For you to be able to kick and fly magically around. That would sort everything out for you, Viggo. You could impress people with your flying and sword skills. Oh, dear readers, how we wish that Viggo could be sitting on a plane bound for China right now, leaning his head against the window and thinking about his life, which has been like this and this and this, but now will be *this*, *this*, and *this*. Mentally preparing to turn his life around, that's what he would be doing. We would like him to be picked up at the airport in Beijing and driven to some steps deep in the forest, a long flight of steps he'll have to ascend to meet the kung fu master who will train him with steely discipline. Viggo would have to go up and down this long flight of steps several times a day to get water from the forest, but he'll understand that it's all part of his training, and so pick up the bucket and start his descent.

•

It would be hard, and the metal handle on the bucket would cut into the palm of his hand, and his feet would start to bleed, but the light in the Chinese valley would be so beautiful that it would fill him with hope, and the thought that this is all part of the purification process, this will make me stronger. And each time he would descend into the shadows with the bucket, there would be less and less light at the top of the steps as evening fell, and he would think: so this is what purification is like. You have to go down and down into the shadows. Your palm hurts more and more. But when the little evening light that was left hit the orange bucket, the water in it would sparkle like a lump of amber, and he would think: I am free.

•

And so the days would pass. He would learn one trick after another with dogged patience: to punch his hand through a brick wall; to lift himself up from the ground on one finger, stretching his body up from this single fingertip; to fly between soft green trees. He would become a completely different person, with a completely different life.

•

Oh, how we wish you could have all this, Viggo! But, instead, here he is, standing in the chapel basement in 1998, trembling.

7

Trine has been down to Kaffebrenneriet and bought herself a large latte and a blueberry muffin, which she's already eaten. She's gotten undressed again and put on her dressing gown, and now realizes that this is what she wants to do, more than anything: to sit in bed with a paper cup between her hands while Oslo—the capital city of Oslo, which she'd thought she would get such a buzz from, now that she's here on her first trip without Haldis—Oslo can just stay shivering outside her hotel window. She's deeply disgusted by herself: all of a sudden she feels it, that she's so *bored* of herself and her drastic and sarcastic ways of flaunting her sexuality, especially when she's doing it on the back of a relationship in which sexuality had been very much at the forefront, as a way of sneering at the relationship, and at herself. These ploys, these exaggerated gestures—tongues lolling out of mouths, figs rubbing against clitorises, secrets painted with gin and vaginal juice on paper—doesn't it all just feel like meat that's become too dry to chew, doesn't her mouth just feel tired of all this chewing, isn't her body rejecting all that dried meat, isn't her body gagging and forcing her mouth to spit it all out, despite the fact that the dry meat is actually her own tongue? Yes.

•

Her phone rings. It says Wanda on the screen. The very same Wanda whom we saw earlier sweating in Frognerparken, lying in her teenage bedroom smoking, is now calling Trine. What links Wanda and Trine together in this universe is a very liquid evening at the end of a theater studies course they both took when they were students a number of years ago, when they drank each other under the table, quite literally: they lay under the table and discovered that there were many reasons why the two of them, out of all the people in the class, should be so attracted to each other, as friends, that is: they were both die-hard fans of PJ Harvey, and they both thought that most other girls were uninteresting and all seemed to be kind of *unaware* of their androgynous potential. Wanda would definitely choose Tracey Emin over Karen Kilimnik's glitter palace any day, but *her* favorite piece from the "Post-feminist Art" exhibition would actually be Sarah Lucas's *Self Portrait with Fried Eggs*, where the artist is sitting leaned back in a chair, in a rather masculine way, with a fried egg on each breast. And that very same Wanda is now phoning Trine, and the name Wanda flashes on the display four times before Trine pulls herself together and answers. Hi, Trine says. Hello, Wanda replies. Great performance yesterday. Yes, but there wasn't much chance to speak, Trine says. No, you left early, Wanda says. Yes, Trine replies, I had a headache. It was fucking good, what you did, Wanda says. Thanks, Trine says. I mean, Wanda continues, you had just the right distance to motherhood, unlike all the others of your kind. What do you mean by "my kind"? Trine asks. She knows that Wanda hates mothers with buggies in cafés; I mean café moms, Wanda says. It hasn't exactly been used that much, has it, the grotesque side of motherhood, Wanda says. Oh, I don't know, Trine says, thing is, my tits were so full of milk they were bursting and I had to do something about it before the performance I was *actually* going to do, so what you saw was in fact *Desperate Mother Milks Herself in Restroom.* Wanda laughs. If I was going to do something about grotesque motherhood, Trine says, I would have just lain down and given birth, and then wandered around with bleeding nipples under a big hospital gown, and those lovely net panties you get that go up over your sagging belly, and the huge diaper that chafes against your ass and still you leave a trail of wet bloody patches behind you. *That* would have been something. Or I could have created a performance titled *New Young Mother Tries to Welcome Visitors Who Don't Understand How Crap It Is Not to Be Able to Put Your Own Baby to Your Breast When Other People Are Watching.* Wanda laughs. But that's what I thought was so fucking good, Wanda said, that you included that aspect, the reckless in relation to the grotesque. I've just seen *Kill Bill: Vol. 2*, Wanda says, and proceeds to explain what she sees as the main problem with the film, as we've discussed earlier, in other words, that everything The Bride does in film number two is rooted in and justified by the most typical of all female roles, namely, that of being a mother, looking after a child, not least, Wanda says, because she was let down by her partner! So, driven by *maternal instinct*! As though women can't *think*! I don't know, Trine says, she thinks Wanda sounds agitated, and that's quite a heavy analysis for this early in the morning, she can hear that Wanda's on the move, she can hear high heels clacking. Have you bought some new shoes? Trine asks, to get away from the mother discussion, Wanda never wears clacking heels. Yes, Wanda says, almost taken aback, because she hadn't remembered that she was wearing them as she stomped about in her room, she bought them on the way back from running, they were standing there, so red and resilient, in a shop window, they're fucking cool, red patent leather with high heels, Wanda says. They'll look good onstage as well, Wanda adds, I'm breaking them in. Trine hears her take a drag on a cigarette. Where was Kåre then, yesterday? Trine asks. It's over, Wanda says, there's a kind of breeziness to her voice, Trine hears her blowing out the smoke, yep, it's over and it's fine. No doldrums for me. Oh, I'm sorry to hear that, Trine says, that it's finished, I mean, not that you're not in the doldrums, that's good, obviously, Trine says, and thinks: red patent high-heeled shoes, the ability to spot a metaphor is obviously the first thing you lose when you're down! But naturally, she doesn't say that. She feels sympathy, she sympathizes with Wanda and the fact that she, the toughest cookie in the universe, is walking around in red patent high heels indoors, because she's probably totally crushed. Well, Wanda says, it was about time, really. He's an author, I'm a musician, it was never really meant to last. He's forty-three, I'm twenty-eight, our lives are different. *Clack, clack, clack* over the floor. But yeah, we'll have to meet up next time you're here, Wanda says. Yes, we'll have to, Trine repeats, and then they hang up, and Wanda takes off the red shoes because her feet are all sweaty, and Trine touches her tender breasts and thinks it would be good to do a piece about the maternal instinct, which could make you kill without hesitation. Wanda doesn't understand. Wanda, Trine thinks, quite obviously doesn't have painful breasts bursting with milk. She leans against the wall briefly and feels how hard and sore her breasts are. She has to do it again. She has to milk herself. She has to find a small bottle and milk herself. She wonders if Wanda will ever experience this, if Wanda will ever have bleeding nipples because they've been sucked by a newborn, and will develop black scabs over her nipples, like a revolting cock's comb, welding all the small channels in the nipples together and stopping the milk from coming out, and if she'll ever stand in the shower with her hands cupped over her breasts so the water jet won't hit her nipples. If Wanda will sit on the edge of the bed the day after she's given birth, and stare at her legs, the naked shins and thighs, and think that they look so thin and defenseless, on the hospital bed, sticking out in that way, from under the big hospital gown that rasps against her nipples, her legs pointing down at the floor. And if she'll pad around in the big hospital gown, which all new mothers wear, when she finally manages to walk without fainting, pad around without any trousers or socks on, because she can't bear to put on her trousers and socks, she can't bear anything, even though they're encouraged to wear their own clothes when they leave the wards and wander around in the hospital corridors so that they don't look like demotivating wrecks for the mothers who haven't given birth yet, if she'll look at herself in a mirror and see an unknown creature, as though she's something the wind just blew in through the window, and then, suddenly, be a mother pushing a sleeping, newborn baby, whom no one knows at all, but who has tiny white milk spots on its nose, down the corridors in a clear plastic crib, a freshly hatched mother who is almost invisible in her huge gown, with the exception of her bare legs and thighs poking out from underneath.

8

Kåre says: the best picture actually comes later in the article, and shows Bush Senior and Junior on a fishing trip, father Bush is standing behind son Bush; father Bush has his arm around son Bush, who's wearing an orange life jacket with reflective strips on the sleeves. Sigrid's response to the description of this picture is: hmm. It's really about father Bush governing son Bush's government, Kåre says, but that's less important to him since what he's writing about, or is going to write about, is a son's not being able to manage without his father, even when he's the president of the United States. It's like there's two parallel stories, Kåre says, but all we can focus on is Sigrid's face right now as she sits there listening to what he's saying: she's listening so attentively that we almost can't keep a straight face. There's something strangely expressive about her, about all of her, even her hair seems to bend out of her head with interest and is, in its imperceptible, hair-like way, completely absorbed by what Kåre is saying, though, at the same time, she's a little nervous she might not give the right response here, navigating a topic she's not a hundred percent certain about—American presidents, that is. For some reason, the names Nixon, Hoover, and Eisenhower always make her nervous. She hopes those names won't crop up in the course of the conversation!

•

Kåre's father never comforted Kåre, Kåre says, he generally just sat in the cellar and drank. And now Kåre is trying, for the first time, with this book, to understand the reasons for that cellar existence. Kåre's mother was a successful seamstress with porcelain skin and a poodle who was jealous of Kåre, and who was fed dog biscuits, like they do in American films to show how spoiled a dog is. You know, dog biscuits that are shaped like the bones you see in Disney films, doggy treats that the little dog snaps out of his mother's hand. Kåre laughs. It's absolutely true. Sigrid laughs, but she thinks that maybe it isn't the right reaction, she should perhaps have said something that might help, or show that she sympathized with his childhood, because she can see, even when he's laughing, that he has a bitter expression on his face. It sounds . . . she starts, her body is limp with sympathy and she wants to comfort him, but Kåre waves this off, back to literature! he shouts cheerfully, and throws open his arms like a circus ringmaster announcing the next act, looks at her with eagle eyes, she thinks all of a sudden, without ever having *seen* an eagle's eyes, but there's something very intense about them, something dark, something helpless, indeed, something *beseeching*, yet closed off at the same time. Sigrid thinks she should almost take the time to make a note of all this, because she has to remember it all when she writes about it later: "dark," "helpless," "beseeching," "closed off," she's never seen eyes like that before. "The Look" is what she thinks she'll call the poem. And she'll be in the poem herself, as someone who's split in two as one half is sucked into the eyes and the other is cast out into nothingness! In a sudden rush, she knows it's going to be a really good poem.

•

Dark, helpless, beseeching, and closed off: we can vividly picture Kåre's mother's porcelain hand holding a Disney-bone biscuit and the small, snapping mouth of a poodle with horrible light pink gums around tiny, sharp teeth that open and gobble down the biscuit while its eyes are fixed on Kåre (eleven). Saliva runs out of the poodle's mouth in slow motion, slimy and shiny. But *ultimately*, Kåre (forty-three) continues, the novel will be about how to deal with yourself and strive to be a better person. Whether you're the son of an American president or the rest of us. (Especially for Kåre, but he doesn't say that.) How to get by without reflective strips on our sleeves, or someone to show you how to hold a fishing rod. That's it. It's simple. But what Kåre finds so fascinating is that dealing with yourself can have global political consequences. And now we're at the heart of Kåre's social/humanitarian project, and we're also at the heart of what Kåre believes is the relationship between ourselves and the world: if George W. Bush had stood up alone, if he had taught himself to fish, it would have had international political consequences, Kåre reckons. And that's where this book comes in, he says, and pulls out *Golf Can't Be This Simple*. Listen to this, Kåre says, and reads: "You see, the only way to really change your swing and your golf game is to change your internal 'picture' of the swing and the game. You cannot make any real changes by trying to directly change what your body is doing. *Real* improvement can only happen from the inside out, *never* from the outside in. *We know* your perfect swing and your perfect golf game are within you *right now*. Let's go find them so you can really enjoy the game." If only, Kåre says, with a lopsided, satisfied smile, Bush had learned some simple, humanistic golf tricks, the world would be a different place. Sigrid smiles. I like the thought that I have the perfect swing and the perfect game in me, at this very moment, Sigrid says. It's never occurred to me before, that somewhere deep down, I play perfect golf, with a perfect swing. Let's go find them, Kåre says, and when they look at each other after he's said this, it suddenly takes on a different, much deeper meaning given the situation they're in, as a man and a woman, and the look between them becomes quite charged.

9

Linnea, on the other hand, is sitting with her head against the car window and looking out at Copenhagen, thinking she would like to live here, she would like to move here and live here, and eat a Danish breakfast every morning and go to a café with orange awnings and red leatherette chairs and round yellow ceiling lamps, like the one where she went with Göran one morning, where you had to put a cross by your choice of white bread, a roll, or rye bread on the menu, and whether you wanted orange juice, apple juice, carrot juice, or tropical fruit juice, and whether you wanted a boiled egg, scrambled eggs, or poached eggs—Linnea thought it was fantastic, and remembers how they crossed off roll, tropical fruit juice, and scrambled eggs. And there it is! The small café with orange awnings and red leatherette seats and round yellow ceiling lamps appears alongside the taxi, and without thinking she turns eagerly to Robert to say "There it is," but as she turns she sees that it's Robert and not Göran who's sitting there, and Robert has nothing to do with this, and she wants to turn back before he's seen that she's turned toward him, but too late, Robert looks at her with a kind expression on his face and says: yes? Oh, nothing, she says, and waves her hand with a smile before turning back, and Robert feels a happiness grow in his stomach, she turned toward him, she said "Oh, nothing," as though she was embarrassed that she'd bothered him, and he takes that to be a very good sign.

•

They've now driven past the café, and Linnea leans forward so she can keep in sight of it, but then they drive around a corner, and it's gone, swallowed as suddenly as it appeared, Linnea thinks. Just as suddenly as Göran had appeared in her life, was there and was manifest and tangible, and just as quickly as he too had been swallowed again by the world, and she hadn't heard from him since. But today, exactly two years later, on January 10, he might be there, standing in front of the glass display case with mummies inside when she (without Robert in tow: she'll suggest that he has a coffee in the Winter Garden while she looks around on her own) comes into the room.

•

(For your information, Göran is, at this moment, almost falling down the stairs into his front hall, clutching his briefcase with the loose pages of his *Don Quixote* lecture bouncing around inside and knocking against its leather walls: he's bounding down the stairs two at a time, heading for the door, heading out onto the driveway where the car is waiting for him—his wife, shivering in her nightgown, took it out for him as he threw on his suit and scooped the lecture up into his briefcase, and now he's pulling open the car door without even noticing that the January sun is sparkling on his newly polished blue Volvo, throwing the briefcase down onto the passenger seat and turning the key: but the car doesn't react. He tries again, but nothing happens. What the hell! Göran shouts, Lotta! he shouts through the door, but his wife is in the shower and doesn't hear, and the car is clearly dead as a dodo. And Göran is extremely late for his lecture, the students have probably already settled into the auditorium, he has to ring the institute and ask them to say he'll be half an hour late, but that the lecture will take place as planned, and now he's got to find his bike: Göran Fältberg runs toward the garage.)

•

Robert and Linnea's taxi pulls sharply onto the side of the road. I check, the driver says as two pearls of sweat run down his temples, I don't think he knows where he's going, Robert says, I think we've been driving in circles, I think we should ask him if he knows where he is. The driver signals with his hand for them to wait, I check, he says again, gets out of the car and walks a short way down the street as he looks up at the buildings. Is he looking for a street sign? Robert wonders and Linnea leans forward to check. The driver comes back with a look of bewilderment in his eyes. Are we lost? Robert asks, with a friendly smile. You take new taxi, the driver says, me no find, he says, and wrings his hands in the air to show that the GPS is not working or has vanished, and then he shrugs, very sorry, very sorry, very sorry! It's quite all right, Robert says, no problem, we understand, don't worry. You get new GPS, he tells the driver, as simply as he can, so he'll understand, then he gives the man a hundred kroner.

No no no, says the driver, and wants to give it back, a small contribution for your GPS, says Robert, holding up the palms of his hands to show that he has no intention of taking the money. Thank you, thank you, says the driver, and Linnea smiles at him as he pulls back out into the road, I wonder if he'll find his way back to his dispatcher, Linnea says, and takes Robert gently by the arm, you were very kind. Robert looks down at her, she's about half his size, and says well, imagine how he must have felt, new job and everything, as he puts up a hand to hail a free taxi that's driving toward them.

10

Sigrid realizes, with a stab in her stomach, right in the middle of the sexual tension that's so suddenly arisen, that the connection between the picture of Bush and one's "inner game" corresponds exactly to the connection she'd experienced that morning between Sofia Coppola, so fluid and fragile, and the aesthetics of *Lost in Translation*, *likewise* fluid and fragile, and thus the incredible possiblity that what one can see on the inside *can* in fact be expressed physically on the outside. She opens her mouth and feels nervous, all of a sudden, but before she's managed to say a word, Kåre says: that thing about *the inner game* is actually pretty spot-on, even though I like to make fun of it. It's true not only for golf but for everything. For example, the book's advice on how best to hit the ball out of a hazard is to imagine it first. *Imagine* the sound of the ball leaving the sand. There shouldn't be much sand in the sound, it should be clean, quiet, poffff, Kåre says, with just a hint of sand. When one has imagined the sound and knows what one is aiming for, one's aim is better. Just as he's about to say what this means in terms of real life, what it illustrates or teaches us, and in particular, the fictitious Bush Junior character and his views on international politics, just as he's about to say this, which also happens to be exactly when Sigrid has finally straightened up her body and mustered the courage to tell Kåre her thoughts on Sofia Coppola and Coppola's inner and outer expression, they hear an almighty bang outside the window and both turn around. A black car has driven into a blue car outside the multistory parking garage opposite the café where they're sitting. The blue car was turning out of the garage, the black car was turning into the street where the blue car was coming out. The blue car had obviously misjudged the turn and now has its nose in the black car to prove it. The doors open and a couple of men leap out. Hands punch the air. Fingers point at the damage to the cars. Oops, says Sigrid. How bizarre. And as Kåre watches the men gesticulate about the collision, he thinks this is crash number two, that he's witnessed *two* crashes since he met Sigrid, that means something, and he is overcome with the grim thought that what it might mean is that he's lost *the inner game*, he was supposed to control himself, *that* is what it means; he was supposed to hear the sound of him and Wanda forever, he was supposed to hear the sound of Wanda getting out of bed before him and going to the kitchen to read the paper and make coffee, he should have heard that sound every morning and held on to it, and not be sitting in a café looking into Sigrid's brown eyes, which have green rings around their irises, and because he's now lost in the thought that he's lost *the inner game*, he doesn't hear Sigrid say enthusiastically that what they're seeing now *is the kind of situation that Daniil Kharms, a Russian author she adores, uses to portray the absurdity of existence, like watching someone gesticulate in a telephone booth!* An image, she adds, that Albert Camus also used in *The Myth of Sisyphus*, where it says . . . um, something about . . . um, what was it again . . . Sigrid tries to remember how it goes; no, she can't remember.

•

But, she says, not many people know that it was *actually* Daniil Kharms who wrote about it first!

11

We'll just pause the second crash for a moment to go back and think about the old woman who crashed into the big van earlier on. She's crashed into a van, she's waved away some ladies in white coats, but what no one knows, other than us, is that this is the last day of her life. And yet she's not going to play a bigger role in this novel than that, she's just going to float in the water, just like the novel's own little log. All she does is wave off some ladies in white coats and then: disappears from the story, which is quite symbolic, really, given that the day we meet her, this day, is the day that she dies. So what about this old lady? What about this old lady's *entire life*? What about the fact that she's taught French grammar at the University of Bergen ever since she got her degree, that she likes coffee with brown sugar, that she doesn't have children, that she's sharper than most people and that her specialty is the French *imparfait* tense, which can be translated as the "past continuous," and that she'll shortly have a fatal heart attack in a parking lot, possibly triggered by the stress of crashing into another car, and thus, forever, pass into the *passé simple*, the "simple past" tense? And what about what she was doing early this morning, not knowing that it would be the last time she'd do it, those little, everyday things, like drying herself with a hand towel? What about the fact that the old lady, as she walked to her car to drive into town and find a lot that was slightly out of the way, which was where she was heading when she turned onto the road and hit a reversing van, what about the fact that she was thinking about something she'd dreamed during the night, something very strange: that she was at home in Ørsta, and that it was December and dark and there was snow everywhere. And that she walked down the small pedestrian street with shops on either side, and everything was closed and there were Christmas stars in all the windows and plastic spruce garlands with yellow and red lights strung between the shops on either side. And these crisscrossed the street with their yellow and red lights as far as the eye could see, and she passed a shop she'd never noticed before, a small green storefront squeezed between the other stores, with a sign that said CINNAMON SHOP. And she went over to the window and looked in and saw that it was true, there was cinnamon everywhere. Cinnamon in small glass bottles in the window, cinnamon in small glass bottles and small paper bags on the shelves behind the counter. Cinnamon in kilo bags. Loose-weight cinnamon under the glass counter. How, she thought, does a shop like this survive? Don't people buy cinnamon in the supermarket? Where they can buy whatever else they might need, cookies, coffee, and bread, she thought in her dream as she stood in front of the window. How much cinnamon would you need in different forms and weights to make you go to the cinnamon shop to buy it? This is what the old lady was pondering, very much awake now as she headed to her car for her last drive in this life. What does one say, she wondered as she pulled her car keys out of her pocket, when one goes into a cinnamon shop? I'd like some cinnamon, please? Isn't that obvious? Or should you say: Do you have any cinnamon? No, that would make a mockery of the cinnamon shop. The person standing behind the counter would give you a look that clearly said: Idiot. This is a cinnamon shop: *of course we have cinnamon!* Perhaps, for that reason, it was a silent shop, where there was no need to say anything other than please and thank you, which could be alternated, depending on which transaction was being made (handing over money) (handing over cinnamon) (accepting money) (accepting cinnamon)? The old woman didn't know, but she thought about the feeling she'd had in her dream as she walked away from the cinnamon shop that stood alone in the middle of the pedestrian street, in the December dark one evening in a dream, after closing time, with Christmas stars shining in every direction, and the cinnamon shop's green wooden facade gently illuminated by all the stars: perhaps the cinnamon shop was the only mystery left in this world, and thank goodness for that, thank goodness for the cinnamon shop, thank goodness that it was there, squeezed in between the multitude of other consumer stores, and only sold the one thing, cinnamon, and was so baffling, so utterly baffling, and yet at the same time totally banal and simple and obvious in its existence.

•

Yes, what about that? What about the fact that the old lady was thinking about all this before she died? And, taking a wider perspective, what about the role that such dreams play when you're going to die? What kind of existence could one say they'd had? They've existed, because they've been in someone's head. But they've never been shared with anyone else. They've existed, they were vibrant and vivid in their existence. What happens to the dreams one's had when one forgets them the minute after one's woken? What happens to the dreams one's had and never told to anyone because one dies before one gets the chance? Did they fly out of her, did she forget? Did they fly out of her like small butterflies when her heart crashed, when all that remained of her was a dream about an absurd cinnamon shop, something invisible that disappeared out of her body, along with herself? Sadly, we will never know the answer to these questions.

12

Could one imagine a place similar to the kingdom of death in the *Aeneid*, where rather than bodies or souls, people's dreams were gathered together to shamble around like Virgil's dead? The bad dreams gathered in one place and the good dreams in another? The bad ones sliding, seeking, grieving, seeking, grieving, toward someone about to enter their kingdom (who would that be?), or like those in Elysium, transparent, beautiful, happy, but gliding, gliding all the time in such a way that one can't tell whether they even have feet with which to touch the ground, dreams like almost transparent bubbles floating over the shining ground, with the light from the sky (the sky is opaque and white) shining through them, so that we (whoever we may be) could see them floating past like tiny plays?

•

And would they come gliding toward us (whoever we may turn out to be), happy to see us, happy to be able to show themselves to someone, and play frantically before our eyes on their little bubbles for fear that we might move on without paying attention to their tiny plots and often absurd symbolism? And would some dreams be as beautiful as Dido, who turns away from Aeneas in shame, and who will never, not even here, in the strange and peculiar land of dreams, be able to show themselves to us—dreams that came here to hide, never to be seen, to glide along endlessly, locked into their sorrow at their own existences?

•

Or are dreams like tiny newborn moon jellyfish, which loosen from their polyps at the bottom of the sea and pulse their transparent way up through the layers of water, until we can no longer see them from where we're sitting on the seabed with our faces upturned, with our tightly closed mouths and our blinking eyes that bulge slightly because of the pressure, and the tiny bubbles that fizz around our noses and mouths and our hair floating back and forth in front of our faces like seaweed as we sit there and try to fathom their origins?

13

And now: back to what's happening outside the café where Kåre and Sigrid are sitting. The black and the blue cars have to move because they're blocking traffic, so the men drive into the multistory parking garage. Sigrid feels embarrassed, cut off, because she's spoken too fast and enthusiastically about the fact that it was Daniil Kharms and not Albert Camus who first wrote about the absurdity of seeing someone gesticulating behind glass, and because Kåre's reaction was only to stare absentmindedly out the window. But she feels that it's important that she be independent and bold, and that she doesn't allow herself to be put off by his lack of response and lack of attention. So she leans back in her chair and decides to relax. He sits there, looking out—and he should be allowed to do so. She tries to find something else to think about.

•

At first she can't think of anything to think about. She just thinks about how uncomfortable it feels that they're not saying anything, and that Kåre is sitting with his face turned away from her. She's very conscious of her hands, her heart is thumping. The arteries in her neck are pulsing. She puts her hands to those arteries, holds them there. It feels like a pretty natural thing to do. She thinks that it all feels totally unreal. They've seen two crashes in one day. She thinks about the old lady with white hair who waved off the other women who came running—how determined she seemed.

•

But there it stops. She can't think of anything more to think about. So she thinks about the planes they saw flying over-head, that they'd both thought the same thing, about all the people inside the plane they knew nothing about. This makes her think about the planes that crashed into the Twin Towers in New York. She thinks how strange it is, that the TV sta-tions never seem to tire of it, of showing the exact moment when the planes plowed into the towers. She sits with her face to the window and thinks with relief that she now has something to think about. It's almost beautiful, she thinks, the way they barrel in, it almost looks as though they're just slipping through, as though there's no resistance in the con-crete, as though flying through a building is something one can easily do, the material all looks so incredibly soft. And it's simply impossible to imagine that there's anyone inside the planes, that there's anyone inside the towers. Now and then she's wondered if the nose of the plane remained intact when it crashed into the concrete, if the nose of the plane hit anyone and pushed anyone farther into the building, through all the walls and out the other side. It's true, she thinks, she should be ashamed. Because it's not particularly nice to think about things like that when it's a matter of someone's life and death. And then out of the blue she remembers a scene in *Mrs. Dalloway*: there's a plane flying up in the air, and Mrs. Dalloway has gone out to buy flowers for a dinner she's hosting later that evening, and Mrs. Dalloway looks up at the plane, and sees that it's making letters with its vapor trail or whatever it is they use, and anyway, something is written in the sky, in the wake of the plane, and Mrs. Dalloway tries to interpret what she sees, and when the narrator then tells us what other people who see the plane are thinking, we discover that they all read what's written in the sky differently. And it's incredible, so incredibly beautiful, Sigrid thinks, because they try to decipher the message letter by letter, but then they all think that the trails look like different letters, and they say the letters out loud: *K*, *R*, or *T* . . . *F*, and they make different suggestions like "Glaxo," "Creemo," and "Toffee." And it's so lovely, Sigrid thinks, because you realize that what one person believes is an *R*, someone else thinks is an *F*, and so on. And that says everything about interpretation! How she, the reader, might also see a letter *R*, whereas someone else reads the letter as *F*, not seeing the small curve that makes *F* into *R*. And how the plane writing the letters has a purpose for writing what it's writing, how it's trying to write a particular word. And how the people who see the plane from the ground, and try to understand, manage to read something into its message, but perhaps not *the meaning* of the word it's trying to write. And how, at the same time, there's something claustrophobic about it all, that inside the plane there's a pilot whom the people on the ground know nothing about, can't see, in the same way that he can't see straight into the brains of the people on the ground—since they're covered by hair and crania—a few hundred feet down below. It's the log again, the floating log, black and waterlogged and unthinking in the middle of an unthinking lake! It sends shivers down her spine. Kåre offers a penny for her thoughts and with great relief she tells him what she's been thinking about, first the Twin Towers and the apparent softness of the collision with concrete, and about the plane in *Mrs. Dalloway* that says everything there is to say about interpretation. She talks quickly and enthusiastically, and explains in detail about *K* and *R* and *T* and *F*, but when she looks at Kåre, she sees that he has an odd expression on his face. So that's what you think about in connection with the planes that crashed into the Twin Towers, Kåre says, and she blushes. Interpretation? he says. Literature? The aesthetics of the apparent softness of the collision with concrete? Sigrid feels a painful knot in her stomach. You've misunderstood, she wants to say, that wasn't what I meant, what I meant (and what about you, who goes on and on about how the one Bush has reflective stripes on his arms and the other doesn't! But she doesn't dare say that), what I meant was—

•

In an *ideal* world, Sigrid would say exactly what she thinks, that this is too much, that, all things being equal, they don't really know each other, even though they have in some way touched each other deep down, through his book and her reading of his book, I mean, Sigrid would say, and yes, I'm ashamed that that's what I think about. She wants to shout fuck. Who is he to come and line her up against the wall? What has she done to him, what's his problem? But she just

becomes smaller and smaller under his scornful gaze, and by
the time he says well, one can think so many things, she's so
small that she almost can't see him anymore, her fingers
stretch up toward the wineglass that's almost out of reach on
the table and it nearly tips over the edge.

•

I don't deserve that reaction, Sigrid says, eventually. There is
silence between them in the café. They're the only guests
now, as the two old ladies, who were sitting below with a cup
of coffee and piece of cake each, have left. The room feels
airy, enormous, blue, full of high windows, and Sigrid is a
guest with a very red face. It's actually quite ridiculous that
such a big, posh café should be so empty. The two waitresses
behind the counter down below are standing talking to each
other, they lean against the countertop behind them, with all
the wineglasses on the shelf above and a mirror behind. A
chandelier hangs from the ceiling, which in many ways resembles an astronomical body in abstract, geometric form,
re-created with silver wires reaching out to become one enormous star, with tiny electric bulbs positioned at just the right
distance from each other, so that the overall effect given by
this astronomical body is in fact that of a beautiful, modern
chandelier. That's all there is in the room, other than a red-
faced Sigrid and a Kåre, who's looking at her—what she's just
said is worthy of respect, and she grows again in his eyes.
Okay, Kåre says. Sorry. I think, he says, that I'm just a bit overwhelmed by you. At the same time that I'm thinking that
you're too good to be true. I'm having problems dealing with
it. I guess I was just trying to pick holes in things. He shrugs,
palms up. Not very nice. I'm sorry. I'm not too good to be

true, Sigrid says, well, maybe a little. Kåre laughs, he likes the fact that she's funny and forthright! It makes him feel confident again, and again he takes her hands. I'm overwhelmed by you, he says, and looks at the table, and as he says it, he hears himself saying it, is overwhelmed by the sound of his saying "*I am overwhelmed by you*," the fact that he's actually *saying* this to someone overwhelms him to the point that tears almost well up in his eyes, because it has to be true then, that he's overwhelmed by someone, by her! And it's all a bit much, really, he says. It doesn't fit with my life. You don't fit. And yet you're so right. Well, now I've said it. Strange, isn't it? Kåre says, and looks back at the table. But I'm overwhelmed by you too, Sigrid says, and hears how stupid it sounds when she says it, partly because she's saying exactly what he said, but also because these are words she seldom says, because they're too big for her mouth, and when she says them her voice gets all distorted and awkward as it tries to sneak past those words. It's all very strange, Kåre says. What do you think we should do about us? Kåre asks. Become lovers, Sigrid says. He snorts and laughs. Right, that would be simple enough, he says. I've already got a girlfriend, Kåre says. Or had, we've kind of split up. Kind of, Sigrid says. Kind of, yes, Kåre repeats. Sigrid looks out the window. It somehow doesn't matter that he kind of has a girlfriend. He's sitting here now with her hands in his. She has to win him over. We could kiss, Sigrid says. Kåre looks at her. He likes the fact that she surprises him like this! Or maybe we can just hold hands, she says, since we already are. Kåre strokes her hands with his thumbs. Yes, you're right, Kåre says. You've got lovely hands, Kåre says, I'm just inspecting them. Ah, Sigrid says, and even though she thinks this is possibly the biggest cliché one could use when sitting in a romantic situation holding someone's hands, she feels giddy and in love. Kåre wants to kiss her. It would be so easy! Then it would all be over and he would go back to being himself. And he could start anew, again. Then Wanda and all her chaos would finally be a closed chapter, and he could start on an unwritten one. Not least, he could admit to himself that he was capable of it, that he *could* hurt the person he loved most. That's just the way he was. And by *admitting* precisely that, and by kissing Sigrid, he could perhaps move on, Kåre thinks as he looks down at Sigrid's hands.

14

Meanwhile: What's happening on the seabed off Greenland? Well, under a layer of mud are some small mussels, their soft innards well protected by the two halves of the shell that are held together by a large muscle, and they lie there, a bit like small forgotten dreams in a fuzzy yet waking brain. Then three heavy walruses with enormous white teeth come swimming through the water. Their lips are gently pressed back by the resistance of the water, as are their whiskers. They dive purposefully down to the seabed and, using their right flippers, start to dig and stir up the sediment that covers the mussels so they can eat the mussels in the following way: holding a mussel firmly between their lips and sucking out the contents—which one could say were the very mussel itself—the soft core, through the opening that mussels, unfortunately for them, have at one end. Then they spit out the shell.

•

And there! We see jellyfish being born! Or that is to say: jellyfish pulling themselves loose and thus starting their lives as unique individuals. But goodness, what a beautiful sight. Minute moon jellyfish stacked up on top of one another, like piles of plates attached to stones which then come loose one by one and pulse and swim up through the water, creating a swarm of moon bubbles, up and up, in the opposite direction from that a duckling might take on its first solo journey in this world, in other words down, down from the nest where they live high up in a tree, bizarrely enough, which they literally have to *fall out* of, one by one, and fall and fall and fall several feet down to the ground, before landing, hopefully, on the soft forest floor. There's a whispering in the water. Something is about to happen, you can feel it. Then the water seems to part as a smooth, streamlined gray Greenland shark glides past, casting us a cursory glance with one eye. It's strange how sharks' eyes always look dead, and yet register the slightest movement. For example, the slightest movement of a salmon that's swum all the way from a small river in northwestern Norway, hung around Greenland for a couple of years, and is now on its way back to the river to spawn. If it weren't for a shoal of herring that appears out of nowhere, and glitters around the salmon as only a herring shoal can, the salmon's days would have been numbered: the Greenland shark simply opens its mouth and glides happily through the shoal, sucking in the herring, and when the salmon is pulled in by the undertow caused by the shark's mouth, it bumps into a mouthful of herring, there's no room for the salmon in the shark's mouth, which closes slowly around the herring; the salmon musters all its strength and wiggles away, slips out, and with a thumping salmon heart swims a good distance along the seabed near Greenland, never noticing that the seabed looks like piles of books, that the lava that once upon a time escaped through cracks in the seabed has been wedged in and pressed down a bit like when you press books into an already full bookshelf. It's amazing; the rocks that can be found on the seabed here are more than 3.8 billion years old, and thus we can find out more about the origins of life here than anywhere else in the world. One theory is that life simply originated on Earth and that those early life-forms used photosynthesis to survive. It's *not* easy to find evidence of the earliest stages of the world, however, because exactly 3.8 billion years ago the entire planet was being peppered by large and small meteoroids from space, and in addition, all the stones from this period have melded with others over the intervening years. But here on the seabed in Greenland there is a small piece of that world that's been preserved, we're talking about the world's oldest stone! And when the stone was studied, large amounts of carbon were found that originated from living organisms. The investigations also showed that the seawater in this vicinity contains some free oxygen from 3.7 billion years ago. Which goes to show that our planet from very early on was teeming with life that breathed in carbon dioxide and spat out oxygen. This tipped the chemical balance of the world and sped up the erosion and shaping of the landscape. And that's why we can say that the large amounts of carbon dioxide here indicate that what we simply have to call "life" (a staggering singular noun for something that's by no means singular in its indefinite infinitude!) had already discovered photosynthesis and so was able to use energy from the sun. But now we have well and truly digressed, even though it's a beautiful thought: that we're extremely close to *the essence of life* here, the answer to a couple of humongous mysteries, but unfortunately we've only brought along a limited amount of oxygen to sustain us for our stay on the seabed and must concentrate on our *real* reason for being here: to see the salmon swim, with its in-built navigation system, all the way home to its small river in northwestern Norway, where the fishmonger's daughter's father is standing one Sunday, his only day off, in 2002, fishing for salmon. And this marks the end for the salmon. Having been born in this very river, then having left and having swallowed en route the gold tooth that flew out of Viggo's mouth in 1998 and fell down a drain and was washed out to sea and finally into the salmon-in-question's mouth, and then having swum all the way to Greenland, and then having lived around Greenland for a few years, and survived the Greenland shark's happy mouth along the way, and then having swum back to the same river where it was born, to spawn, it now opens its mouth wide for a tempting, shimmering silver thing, the fishmonger's daughter's father's bait, a pretend fish, and tugs back as hard as it can when it feels its mouth being pulled up toward land. It pulls back, deeper into the river, away, away, away! but is then hauled in, and is now caught, but doesn't give up for another half hour, until the fishmonger's daughter Elida jumps out into the river and catches it herself, to the fisherman's great delight.

15

Elida also feels great delight. She's been sitting here by the pool all day, while her father has been fishing and fishing, she's been sitting in the shade under the tall trees by the mill and reading Dante's *Divine Comedy* (it's the absolute truth! she is the *third* person in this book to read Dante's *Divine Comedy*!), even though she's only sixteen years old. When she's been reading for a long time, she takes a break as she thinks she deserves to daydream for a bit, she dreams of being lifted up into Viggo's strong arms, a dream she's had since the funeral, where she stood with her tongue out so he could look into her mouth, he was so handsome and so big, and in her dreams he lifts her up and whispers urgently in her ear that he loves her, and she feels her breasts pressing against his rib cage, and then he kisses, kisses, kisses, and kisses her. Kisses, kisses, and kisses. And then: back to Dante's *Divine Comedy*. She likes it, she likes reading books that the others in her class don't want to read. Whenever she sees a book that's thick and looks difficult, with an unattractive cover, she jumps on it. And today, in the heat of the sun while her father fishes and fishes (something that's touched her whenever she's looked up from her book, that he, a fishmonger, should choose to spend his day off fishing, he must have a very strong and sincere feeling for fish, she thought, this man who is her father, she's seen him standing there in the pool in his waders that go all the way up to his groin and watched him concentrate and look around for hours without catching a fish, and it moved her, because it gave her a deep sense that *this is her father*, the fishmonger), she's been sitting in the shade and reading about what awaits those who betray their family and country, in hell—namely, to be trapped in a frozen lake. What's also moved her is the idea that seven hundred years ago a man sat and wrote this, that the following verse, written seven hundred years ago, could make her arms freeze, and make the small hairs on her arms stand up like a see-through forest:

> At this I turned and saw a frozen lake spread
> Before me and beneath my feet, looking more
> Like glass than water. Even in the dead
>
> Of winter, the Danube in Austria never wore
> A veil of ice as thick as this, nor did the Don
> Under its frigid sky support what this lake bore.

And this:

> And as to croak the frog doth place himself
> With muzzle out of water,—when is dreaming
> Of gleaning oftentimes the peasant-girl,—

Livid, as far down as where shame appears,
Were the disconsolate shades within the ice,
Setting their teeth unto the note of storks.

Each one his countenance held downward bent . . .

•

Were the disconsolate shades within the ice!!! And when they cried, these souls that were stuck, chin-deep, in the ice in a frozen lake that resembled glass, their tears froze and "the frost congealed the tears between, and locked them up again"! And she was horrified when Dante lost control and grabbed and pulled at the locks of one disconsolate stuck in the ice, he "pulled out more tufts than one," he was so angry with those traitors. And right at the end of Canto 32, he and Virgil see a terrible sight: two men who've been placed in the same hole, one man's head positioned in such a way that he sits like a hat on the other man's head, "his teeth fused to another man's skull." And this man *eats* and gnaws at the other man's skull and brain! These two are Count Ugolino, who's the one gnawing, and Archbishop Ruggieri, who's being gnawed. The archbishop locked the count up in a tower with his two young sons and his two grandchildren, nailed the door shut, and then one by one, the sons and grandchildren starved to death, having offered themselves as food to their father, the father quite literally eating his children and grandchildren: "Though they were dead, two days I called them. Then hunger proved more powerful than grief." And that was why, in death, he sat gnawing on the archbishop's skull, for eternity, in a frozen lake.

•

Elida! A shout in her head as she sat there dumbstruck and imagined this head gnawing at the other's skull in the frozen lake, give me the gaff hook! She looked over at her father, who was standing with his fishing rod bending down toward the water, and it took a few seconds before she understood what the words meant, that her father was a person who needed help to catch a fish, and that she was the person who could help, she was numb in all her joints after sitting tensely reading, but she ran down to the riverbank, grabbed the gaff hook, and shouted: But what do I do now? You have to wait a little, her father puffed, and when you see the fish appear close to the bank, go into the river and hook it. But how do I do that, Dad? she shouted. I haven't got time to show you, her father shouted back, you'll just have to manage. Use all your strength, you have to hit it, preferably just below the head. Huh? Elida shouted over the noise of the water. The head! her father shouted. Elida gripped the gaff hook. She had to manage it, she looked at her father's red face and his arms holding on to the fishing rod, she couldn't let him down now, he'd been standing there all day waiting, she had to hook it, and there was the salmon, and Elida raised the gaff hook and brought it down with all her might, and felt the gaff hook hit the fish and catch—and then you pull it onto the bank! her father shouted, and Elida tried, but it was so heavy, this fish, and how it twisted and turned! Then suddenly her father was there and took the gaff hook from her and threw the salmon onto the bank. And there it lay, flapping, big and shiny, until her father pulled out the hook and bashed it on the head till it was dead. You were great, her father said, smiling, and put his arm around her shoulder and hugged her so

she could smell the salt and sweat on his skin. Well, Elida
said, making a point of not being too pleased about his
praise, but she was trembling all over.

•

And then, an hour later, her father called to her from the
kitchen that she had to come and see, there was a tooth in
the salmon! She thought it was only fitting, that the day should
end with her standing there holding a tooth in her hand, a
tooth that had once been in someone else's mouth, and a gold
tooth at that! Elida couldn't help but imagine how the person
had left the dentist's and gone out to the small waiting room
with flushed cheeks and messy hair and looked in the mirror over the sink and smiled as they saw the new gold tooth
flash. Perfect, the person thought. What if, the thought struck
her, what if Viggo was that person? Imagine if this was the
tooth he had lost down the drain and it had been eaten by a
fish and now come back to her? You can keep it, her father
said, and laughed, you look like you need it, you're looking at
it so intensely. Have you seen the gold cap? Elida asked. Yes,
you could get it melted down and made into a pendant. Isn't
that what happened to someone once? her father said. Someone who was in the sea inside a fish and was melted down
and made into jewelry? The steadfast tin soldier, Elida said.
He only had one leg. Yes, that's right. The tin soldier with
one leg, her father said. They made him into a heart, isn't
that right? Elida felt her stomach flutter. *A heart.* But she
didn't want to melt it down. She wanted to keep the tooth. It
would remind her of the day she sat in the shade and read
about Count Ugolino gnawing on Archbishop Ruggieri, and
how she herself, moments later, hooked the flesh of a salmon.

And then, but she almost couldn't think this, because it would show on her face, it would remind her of Viggo, of being lifted up into his arms and being kissed, kissed, kissed, kissed, and kissed. She turned away from her father and closed her eyes. She imagined she was walking toward Viggo, saying: I've had your tooth all the time. And Viggo would say: and I love you.

}

16

Ten years later, she's not so fixated on the kissing anymore, but she does still have the tooth in her pocket, and as she stands there on the Charles Bridge over the river Vltava that runs through Prague, she suddenly has such a powerful sense of *time* that she has to hold on to the gray stone that the bridge is made from. She feels faint as it suddenly strikes her that every second that passes is like a bite, that time is eating at her, that time is eating away at her insides in the same way that time has gnawed at this bridge and worn it down, worn down the stone under her hands and worn down the black, pointed statues that line the bridge on either side and cast frightening black silhouettes in the water, and farther upon the hillside, the big castle, which looks inaccessible with its high, long walls and endless dark windows. She has to close her eyes and just hold the stone that the bridge is made of and listen to the sounds around her, the sound of how sudden this all is, how *here and now* it is, how here and now and *sudden* this bridge is, even though it's stood here and stood here for several

hundred years, how sudden and eternal *everything* is, that
that's what *time* is, *this is time*, Elida thinks, and feels the tears
pressing against her eyelids and escaping out the corners, she
has to fumble in her pocket for the tooth, which she always
carries with her, the tooth with gold in it, she has to hold it
up, open her eyes, and look at it. The gold is dull, but it's still
gold, and gold, thinks Elida, is everlasting. And teeth, thinks
Elida, are just as everlasting as our bones! But the flesh on the
fingers that hold the tooth up to the sky, that much is not
eternal, though it feels like it is, though it feels as solid as a
statue's arm, except that it *is* alive, and *will* die. *And I endure
eternally*, Elida thinks solemnly, because of all the lines in the
inscription on the gate to hell in Dante's *Divine Comedy*, it is
this one that always stays with Elida. *Eternal* and *eternally* I
endure, Elida thinks, and suddenly she fully understands
what it *means*, it means precisely the feeling she felt just now,
that the bridge was sudden and eternal at the same time, *to be
eternal* is in a way a contradiction, setting eternity in the
present tense, Elida thinks, since the present tense is to all
intents and purposes a moment-by-moment thing, whereas
the eternal is something that extends beyond the moment,
which is exactly what the bridge does, or what her feeling
about the bridge does, even though it's happening right now!
There's something so absolute about it that it makes her
tremble. Elida, she hears somewhere in her head, shall we go?
She turns and looks at Magnus and feels, for some reason,
irritated—not pleased—to see him here; I've bought puppets, he says, and holds up two marionettes, here, one's for
you. He kisses her on the cheek, and she looks at the puppet
he's bought for her: a ballerina in a light pink tulle tutu. She

wants to cry. He mustn't see the tooth. She slips it back into her pocket. Shall we go to the castle, it's about time we got up there, he says.

•

And Elida really does want to go to the castle. After all, she's going to write about Kafka's *The Castle* for her thesis, for her literature degree, about all the snow that makes it so hard for K to walk there. There's no snow here now, even though it's January, and it's easy for them to move their feet, and if she wants to, well, the castle is right there. And she does have to go up to the castle. She's been looking forward to this trip ever since Magnus came running toward her and shouted: *We're going to Prague!* brandishing the two tickets that he'd just bought without asking her. And the first time she came here to the Charles Bridge she saw the castle in the distance up there on the hill, though nowhere near as far away as in the book, where the castle just looms in the distance as something unreachable, certainly for K, who never gets there, no, it's definitely much closer than that, it's actually only about a twenty-minute walk from the Charles Bridge, twenty minutes at most, but all the same: distant, closed, aloof, especially now with the afternoon clouds reflected in its windows, there are rows and rows of windows with nothing in them, windows that close everything out by reflecting the clouds, and she can't help but believe that it was this castle that Kafka was thinking of when he wrote *The Castle*, but when she looks at Magnus, she realizes that for some reason she doesn't want to go there with him. Her boyfriend. He irritates her, even though they've only been together for a few months, he irritates her already. She says: Can't we wait until tomorrow? My legs are so tired. I can't face it. Magnus looks at her with disappointment. Do you really mean that? You've said that for the past two days, do you not *want* to go there, is that what it is? Yes, honest, I do, Elida replies, but I think we should *start* the day by going up there and not leave it to the end. I get so tired, and I want to be fully awake when I go there. Okay, Magnus says. But let's go first thing tomorrow, then.

•

Elida studies Magnus as he sits eating a pizza inside one of the darkest cafés they could find. Not that they were looking for a dark place. It's just that everything is dark in Prague, Elida thinks, dark and snowless. She looks at his hair, which is always messy, and she thinks that she'll just have to dump him if she feels like this, if she doesn't feel anything, is always just thinking about something else, something else that draws her attention all the time; for example, the castle. The snow. Time. He looks up at her. Are you not going to have anything? I'm not hungry, Elida says. Chin-deep, she thinks, I'm sitting chin-deep in my own frozen lake! That's the problem. At least have a beer, Magnus says. She could, sure, she thinks, gets up and goes over to the bar and orders a beer. There are three big men sitting at the bar talking loudly in Czech, they say something to her and smile, I don't understand, sorry, she says, they point toward Magnus and say something again, and pull out a chair for her, she laughs, no thank you, but that's very kind of you, they laugh and shrug, as though saying, your choice, fair enough, and she goes back to Magnus with a tankard of beer in her hands, she holds it with both hands; I saw that they wanted you to sit with them,

Magnus says. She smiles. I'm an attractive young woman, you know; yes, you are, Magnus says, an attractive and young but tired woman. Could you not get anything smaller? Magnus says, and laughs at the huge tankard.

•

Oh, why can't I just love you, she thinks. Why is snow all she can think of? Snow, snow and ice. And time.

17

Kåre's trip to Bergen has thus turned out to be rather different from what he'd anticipated. He had imagined: traveling
to Bergen, reading for the businesspeople, making them
laugh, receiving (preferably resounding) applause, leaving,
thinking about the contrast between the applause in there
and the quiet outside, back in real life, where everything
would then seem quiet and cold by contrast. But instead, this
happened: he gets his applause, leaves, can't decide where to
go, goes to a café, sits in the café, feels bitter, empty, cold,
stands up abruptly and starts to walk toward Nordnesparken
to find someplace where one can stand and look out and gather
one's thoughts, and then there, at that place, he finds a girl in a
green woolen coat standing with her chin in her hands on the
railing, and he tries not to be bothered, not to think *Jesus* and
just give up, tries to shut everything else out because after all
he must surely be able to stand there even if there's someone
else already there, and he could even glance at her and see
that she's standing there with her chin in her hands, looking

rather desperate, and quite pretty, actually, at which point he would surely be able to say "Nice day for standing with your chin in your hands," or something like that, and be able to look her in the eye . . . And now Kåre's trip to Bergen has taken such a turn that he looks around the café and sees that the two old ladies who were sitting below have left, and that there's no one here that he knows, he doesn't know the waiters, he doesn't know the people walking past the window, and what are the chances that the people walking past would recognize him or know who he is (even though he often gets the feeling that people know who he is), and he leans forward and says, come on then. She leans forward too. Like this? she asks, and puckers her lips. No, not like that, he says, and laughs and leans back. Her face relaxes, leans even farther forward and tries to be normal. Like this then? she asks. No, not like that either, he says, and now it's gone, the beautiful moment is gone. I don't believe you, Sigrid says. Nor do I, he says, and kisses her, briefly, so his lips only touch her lips, no more, but it's a kiss all the same.

18

Kåre. This man who is sitting in a café and has just kissed Sigrid on the mouth—a short but warm kiss. This man who is forty-three years old, and who is to all intents and purposes together with Wanda, but has now kissed another woman, not that it's the first time he's kissed another woman when he's been together with someone else, but it's the first time since he's been together with Wanda, who he is indeed still together with, in some way, even though they're officially taking a break, and who he has until now thought of as his great love, his true harbor and home . . . This man sits there and feels his chest running hot and cold for that very reason. The revelation that this kiss was supposed to be has not revealed itself and what he feels is that if he's never hurt Wanda before, he certainly has now. What is it? Sigrid asks, because she can tell that there's something, there's a strange look in his eyes, and his face darkens, and she wonders absently how that's possible, if it's the blood that's darkened his cheeks, if it's seeping out into the tiny vessels in his skin the way that

thunderclouds slip stealthily across the sky, thus slowly dark-
ening the color of his face, vessel by vessel, and she thinks *aha!*
Is *that* where the expression "his face clouded over" comes
from? It's nothing, Kåre says, I'm just a little surprised that I
did that, since I shouldn't have done it. That should never
have happened.

•

But why did it happen, then, Kåre wonders, what is it that
made that happen, now? Hasn't he in fact been waiting for it
to happen, for him to hurt Wanda in the way that he hurts
everyone, which he's come to the conclusion he does in order
to preempt them hurting him? Which shows him that he's
actually a very sensitive person? Or *is* he just a cynical bas-
tard? And did it actually happen now, when he kissed Sigrid,
or did it not in fact happen before, didn't it actually happen
a week ago when he and Wanda argued about Uma Thurman and he felt that he was simply *over it*? And hadn't they
in fact been gradually drifting apart over the time that
they'd been together, her with all her insecurities, despite her
tough image, which he found so wearying, and he with, well,
his weariness with all the insecurities hidden behind that
tough image? I think it was rather nice, Sigrid says, and Kåre
looks at her and thinks she's so young, she knows so little,
and he's almost moved by her. He puts his hands over hers
again and says sorry, I didn't mean to be melancholy. The
waitress comes up the stairs and puts two steaming bowls of
onion soup down in front of them as well as a small basket of
fresh bread and butter. Mmm, it smells good, Sigrid says.

19

There is the Glyptotek. It stands like an island, more or less, or an oasis, in the middle of all the traffic, in the middle of the asphalt desert, Linnea thinks, and she feels her stomach lurch because she can so clearly see what the opening shot of her film should be: the audience will sit in the cinema in the dark, everything is in blackout, then the sound of the traffic around the Glyptotek will gradually get louder and suddenly the picture will appear, bright and clear on the screen, daylight, in a flash, so one sees the Glyptotek from somewhere out in the middle of the traffic, with cars driving in front, trucks, cyclists, but it won't be obvious in that moment where it is, as the Glyptotek doesn't look Danish, it looks like something one might find in Marrakesh or India or Greece, Linnea thinks, as architectural history isn't her strong point, with its redbrick facade, alcoves, and black statues and domed roof. And then, like a Truffaut film, the camera will focus and zoom in on a girl walking across the square; at first she'll appear small and in the distance, and initially we won't know that the movie is about her, because to begin with she's just part of the bigger picture: but then the camera *zooms in* un- mistakably on her, and we go right up to her and see her standing there looking up at the entrance, the massive, dark wooden doors, before walking up the steps and going in. Linnea grabs Robert by the arm: this is it, this is the open- ing, she says, and tells him to lean forward between the front seats of the taxi and then she shows him where she wants to position the camera, roughly speaking, and how the image will zoom in on the main character who will be walking toward the camera about there.

•

All Robert can think about is the fact that their heads are nearly touching, they almost have to hug, they're sitting so close together to be able to see out between the two front seats of the car. Her flyaway hair brushes his cheek, it tickles.

20

For a few seconds, Kåre feels that he's been cast into darkness, the dark waiting in the big, cold cave that's been sealed off with a steel lock for three years now (the lock=his love for Wanda, a lock he's kind of known wouldn't hold): the cave that he still wishes so desperately would shrink away and disappear if only he didn't think about it, if he could only hold on to Wanda, if only he could convince himself for once that he wasn't the sort of person who ruins everything, if only he could convince himself for once that everything would be fine, that he was capable of keeping something together, that something would finally go right. This is what he'd tried to express in his poetry collection, where the good old-fashioned storytelling, as Sigrid had called it, was entirely a declaration of love, hope, and determination, and it was the *entirety* that was important, that was what he wanted, he was determined to have the *entirety*. But now he has, like Bill in *Kill Bill*, hurt the person he thought he would never hurt. In other words, it *was* greater than him, this darkness that could rear up at the most unexpected times and make him do things he almost hadn't realized he was capable of. And now he'd done it. He'd hurt Wanda with this kiss, this whole encounter with Sigrid, and if he'd thought that he would never do anything like this again in his entire life: well, he thought wrong. And now it's over. If he's had even the smallest doubt in the last week, despite everything: it's now definitely over. It's now definitively clear. He's the same. The same, the same, the same! He picks up his spoon and dips it in the onion soup, stirs it a bit. The onion pieces move around, gently float in new patterns dictated by the movements of his spoon, but he barely notices. Is this the point of recognition from where everything can begin again? he wonders.

•

Sigrid is at a bit of a loss, she's a bit confused right now. Her face sort of resembles that of an eight-month-old baby, when the baby is exposed to a form of adult communication the baby can't yet understand—for example, the adult jumps around on the floor like an idiot in an attempt to entertain the baby, who is taken aback and looks away from the adult, slightly embarrassed, and the baby's face is slack and serious, and it's possible to detect something akin to discomfort there, because the baby knows it *should* understand, but doesn't understand all the same. What do they expect of me? the baby thinks as it looks away. That's what Sigrid's face looks like just now, because she doesn't understand everything that's going on inside Kåre, his thoughts about the cold cave that has quite possibly opened up again as he kissed Sigrid (an event that comes on top of a number of other recent events, Kåre thinks, according to which view the argument about

Kill Bill: Vol. 2 was in fact the culmination of something that had already started, had possibly even started before he was born, perhaps it was in his genes that he would turn out like this, his DNA strands had knotted themselves together with the greatest reluctance and *knew* what would happen), and what that might mean for him as a person. Sigrid tries to eat some onion soup as well. But: she can't lift the spoon of soup to her mouth. It seems to be impossible to get her hand to move toward her mouth, there's no problem lifting the soup halfway up from the bowl, but when her elbow has to move her lower arm up toward her mouth, her underarm starts to shake, and the harder she tries to complete the movement to her mouth, the more violently her underarm shakes, and the soup starts to spill over and fall back into the bowl, and when she eventually thrusts her head forward, like an animal greedily snapping up a piece of meat, because her arm can't complete this movement to her mouth, her face is so red that she's extremely grateful that Kåre is sitting staring down into his own soup and hasn't looked back up yet. She tries again, but the same thing happens, just as her underarm starts to move up and in toward her mouth, her arm seems to lock and she can't get the spoon up to her mouth, it's simply impossible! And almost worse than the first time. When she holds the spoon with both hands, she manages, and if she supports her right arm with her left arm, she can even get the spoon to her mouth without spilling any soup back down into the bowl. But naturally it looks very stupid.

21

It is of some interest to note that the way in which Sigrid is eating her soup is not dissimilar to the way in which The Bride in *Kill Bill: Vol. 2* tries to eat rice, when she's sitting on the floor in that spartan room with the kung fu master Pai Mei, after days of serious hard training and punching her fist into a wooden wall without managing to punch through. The only thing The Bride has succeeded in doing is to use up all the strength in her fingers and arms. Uma Thurman sits there and tries to pick up some steaming rice with shaking chopsticks that she can't even hold between her fingers because she doesn't have the strength, and then she can't get the few grains of rice that she manages to pick up with the chopsticks to her mouth because her arms aren't working. What's interesting is that Sigrid has *not* been through such physical and mental near-torture at the hands of a strict kung fu master with an absurd white beard that he throws over his shoulder, cackling with glee, every time The Bride fails to do what she's trying to do, and yet Sigrid is having exactly the same problems getting food into her mouth. That's how powerfully a person's tense inner life can affect their external physiognomy!

22

The kung fu master's spartan room reminds us of Viggo once again, and our wish that he could go to China to be trained in kung fu. Where is he now? We can't see him anywhere! We look all over his home village, but can't find him. We randomly pick out Bergen too, but don't find him there either. The waterfront in Bergen, Bryggen, at a quarter past twelve, but no Viggo to be seen looking up at the crooked buildings. Nor is Viggo up by the two-spired St. Mary's Church, where Sigrid lives, only Sigrid's not there, she's sitting in a café with large windows trying to get soup up into her mouth. No Viggo to be seen on Strandgaten and no Viggo in Marken. No, he's not here then, is he? We look through all the streets in Oslo, but no Viggo at Oslo S train station, no Viggo on Dronningens Gate, no Viggo on Haxthausens Gate, and in the beautiful light at Slottsparken: no Viggo . . . Nor, for that matter, is Viggo to be seen on Drammensveien, but we do see Wanda there walking along briskly in a pair of bright red high-heeled patent leather shoes, she's listening to PJ Harvey and singing in her head, with a kind of fervent, almost liberating rage: "I wanna chase you round the table, I wanna touch your head!" And this no doubt has something to do with the feeling the red shoes give her, that she's invincible, and that she'll hold out and not call him, she hasn't been in touch with him since she moved back to her mother's, and she hasn't been in touch with him on principle, because "He will call *me*, because if not, *I've* lost," and we see Wanda walking and walking until she can't bear it anymore because of the blisters on her heels, and she puts on the grayish-white Converse sneakers she usually wears and which she's brought along in her bag just in case, but now it's almost as difficult to walk in them as in the heels, because of the blisters, which don't disappear along with the shoes that caused them; we follow her with our eyes, just to be sure, until she swings through the doors of Pascal and hugs a friend who's sitting there waiting with a salad and a pot of tea. We carry on looking for Viggo in Madrid, in London, in Helsinki, in New York, in Barcelona, in Buenos Aires, in Berlin, in Stockholm, as though it were possible that Viggo, in the middle of his personal crisis in the chapel basement, somehow took a great leap out into the world, and then suddenly we realize: we've been looking somewhat prematurely for Viggo in 2008. In 1998, however, all of a sudden we hear a gasp, as though in an absolutely silent room, as though for example the still surface of the ocean was suddenly broken by a person pushing up from the depths and gasping for air, so intensely and so suddenly that it's almost as if the surface of the water was in our head and it was absolutely still until someone gasped for air in our head, between our ears, at which point the only thing we could hear was this gasp, that's how we hear Viggo gasp, and suddenly we see him in a bed in Bergen that we obviously hadn't noticed, at a quarter past nine in the evening. Viggo coughs, reaches for the glass of water standing on the chest of drawers beside the bed, and takes a drink. It turns out that we've found Viggo again just as he's waking from a dream, in 1998, where he was about to throw himself off a cliff and fly over a bright green valley in China, but he woke up just as he was about to jump off. Why couldn't he experience the feeling of flying? He's never dreamed that he could fly, apparently it's a very common dream, but he's never dreamed it. Ståle often dreams about it, but Ståle also smokes dope every now and then, and Viggo doesn't, maybe that's why. Maybe his head just refuses to let him fly in his dreams because it knows that it's beyond his capacity as a human being? That even in his dreams he wouldn't allow it? That even his dreams would be constrained? That he was *that* bad? Viggo sits in bed until he has to stand up to get some feeling back in his legs, he stamps around on the floor, he's naked and stamping his feet on the floor, how long was he asleep? What's he doing here? And why did he dream about China? Is his life so limited that even the small coastal town of Bergen is as exotic as China to him? He looks out, he's never been in Bergen before, but he's come here now. He didn't go back to Oslo. A few hours after his grandmother's funeral, he packed his suitcase and decided he would go anywhere except to Oslo, just not back there where everything had gone wrong. What were his choices? The destinations available at the local airport within the next hour: Sogndal, Florø, and Bergen. Oh, the look in his mother's eyes when she said, after packing frozen portions of stewed apples and blueberry jam in his suitcase, that she hoped he would come home again soon, after which she gave him a copy of Kafka's *The Castle* apparently completely at random and said that perhaps he needed something to read. Had his mother really read it? Is that how you feel, Mom, he wanted to ask, I've never really spoken to you, what are you trying to tell me by giving me *The Castle*, are you K, wading through deep snow trying to get up to the castle, and am I, your inaccessible son, the castle that you can't reach? Have you *read* this, Mom? he asked her, close to tears. No, his mother said sheepishly to the floor, I just picked it out of the bookshelf one day, it had such a lovely blue cover. Viggo gave her a hug and said that he promised to come back again soon. This is what Viggo thinks about as he stands naked at the window, behind the curtains, and knows *finally* that he must try to change his life, he has to close his eyes and feel the dream of the Chinese valley sink into his body, just as dusk will slowly fall and fill the Chinese valley with darkness, we think.

23

Ten years later, he's almost forgotten all this. Viggo (thirty-one) is on his way to the café he runs in Bergen, early one morning in January 2008, and is suddenly reminded of this dream when he sees a kung fu movie on a huge flat-screen in a TV shop window. He stands there watching at nine o'clock one January morning in 2008 as the light naturally and reliably fills the Bergen streets, while the camera pans out over the Chinese valleys and the steep, forested mountainsides. Viggo feels a sigh ripple through his body, then walks on.

•

And the question we obviously have to ask is: Has he changed much, Viggo, over the past ten years?

•

He opens the door to the café, turns on the lights, starts the espresso machine. He sees a man in a dark suit walk by outside and feels his heart skip a beat; the man stops, looks at him, what does he want? Viggo registers that he grabs hold of a knife under the counter, he waits, hand around the knife. The door opens: Are you open? asks the man in the suit.

24

Sigrid decides to hold off on her soup awhile and instead butters a slice of crusty bread, she can't wait to taste it, it's one of her favorite things, fresh bread with butter, only butter, and she manages to get the bread to her mouth without any problem, because she can do it so fast that her arm doesn't have a chance to freeze up and start back in with those concentration-shakes, since there's no soup to be spilled. She perhaps lifts the bread to her mouth a little too fast, but so what! She takes a bite and chews. It's really good. She tries to think that she's having a good time, she's in a café eating delicious bread and butter and it doesn't matter that neither of them is saying anything, that Kåre is sitting looking down at his soup with a grim, grim expression on his face. She tries to think that this will all be amusing to them in retrospect, when they've gotten over the first shock of their first meeting, and that she will laugh when she tells how she struggled to get the soup to her mouth because she was so tense. And now she wonders if perhaps seeing the whole situation from outside like that might have helped her arm to relax, so once again she picks up the spoon, dips it in the soup, and tries to guide it to her mouth. It's simply not possible. It's like her arm has a lock that makes it impossible to get it up to her mouth. She takes a piece of bread and holds it under her spoon, moves it up toward her mouth, maybe that's how she has to eat the soup, with bread at the ready *as soon as* the soup reaches her mouth? People eat soup and porridge in so many different ways. Some people run the spoon around and around the bowl, from the edge inward, others go at it at an angle. She tries to cheer herself up with the thought that this is all at least allowing her to experience herself in an extreme situation, as in "extremely tense"; she tries to cheer herself with the thought that she's experiencing just how tough it can be, those few inches from the supporting bread to her mouth, when the spoon is alone; she tries to cheer herself with the thought that she'll just close her eyes and make a final, desperate attempt to get the spoon in her mouth. When she opens her eyes again, she sees that Kåre is sitting there with tears in his eyes; he laughs, puts his hand around the wrist of the hand that's holding the bread, and lowers it to the table. Sigrid, he says, you can relax, I don't bite. Mmh, Sigrid blows through her nose. I regret ordering the soup, I forgot that my arms stop working when I'm nervous, she says. It always happens; for example, when I've got an oral exam, I can't drink the glass of water that's in front of me. Just be yourself, Kåre says. You don't need to be nervous.

25

No, not tense, not tense in her heart, not tense in her body, not tense in her arms that are supposed to guide the soup to her mouth, nor tense in her innermost core, like the frozen lake in Canto 32 of the *Inferno* in Dante's *Divine Comedy*: "Of winter, the Danube in Austria *never wore* / A veil of ice as thick as this, nor did the Don / Under its frigid sky support what this lake bore" (our italics). A veil of ice as thick as this, Sigrid's shoulders should never bear. Because the thing, the very serious thing, is: if she's nervous, she will eventually lose Kåre's respect. It would have been good for her to know this, because then she might perhaps have worked on it and thus avoided the consequences when she sits down to breakfast in his kitchen one month from now. But she of course doesn't know, currently sitting in the café, that this will happen.

III

DINNERTIMES / EVENINGS / MORNINGS / MIDDAYS / AFTERNOONS

1

Because a month from now, this will have happened: Sigrid and Kåre have kept in touch by email and phone, and the distance between them will in many ways have been beneficial. Whenever they've spoken together, they've been able to stand by their windows, gazing out, and the view, as is often the case from a window—particularly if there are trees outside, and particularly if those trees are slowly being covered by snow that lands falling on their branches (because: if we watch a snowflake land on a branch in slow motion, we see that the snowflake actually doesn't stop falling until both ends of the flake have settled on the gentle curve of the branch, like a hand placed affectionately on an arm, a humble greeting from one natural phenomenon to another, in other words: snowflakes land *falling*), and particularly when it's dusk, or in the glow of streetlamps—the view and the magic it invokes blends with the sense of the person one has just been speaking to—a marvelous consequence for those in love. The person one has spoken to and is in love with becomes, in a way, part of one's sense of self, there by the window, with the snow falling onto the branches. Then, when one has stood by the window and nurtured this good feeling long enough, one can carry on with whatever one was doing, and one can *hold on to* this feeling because the other person isn't there to disturb the image with things other than that magical falling onto trees. If the other person had been there, the image might have been spoiled by the things one does that have no magic about them, such as pulling off one's woolen socks and dropping them on the floor rather than folding them together and putting them in the basket exclusively reserved for woolen socks, or putting the brown goat's cheese back in the fridge after it's been standing on the counter in the kitchen for hours and is all crumbly as a result, or picking one's teeth with one's nail at the same time as making sucking noises, trying to dislodge the food that's stuck right by a wisdom tooth, or disturbing the other person who is, for example, watching TV, by having long telephone conversations with someone else. The distance meant one could avoid all this. One could finish the phone call, look out the window, watch the snow falling down onto the branches, get that magical feeling.

•

And then, one day, a postcard arrived for Sigrid, with a picture of a chair on the front, an ordinary wooden chair, and on the back of the card it said: When are you coming?

2

And here we see Sigrid as she arrives on the street where Kåre lives, in Oslo, in a taxi. It's February, evening, and dark, and she's taken the train from Bergen to Oslo, and it's been snowing so much in Oslo that it's not easy for the taxi driver to turn onto Kåre's street. The cars parked on both sides of the road are blanketed with snow, and the taxi driver goes very slowly. Kåre is standing by his kitchen window looking out, waiting. Both Sigrid's and Kåre's hearts are thudding. They've almost forgotten what the other looks like. The taxi carries on down the street getting closer and closer to Kåre's house and it's only a matter of seconds until Sigrid will lean into Kåre and kiss him on the neck, and, to her horror, get the feeling that the skin of his neck is in her mouth, a sagging fold of skin.

•

Next morning: we see Sigrid's face. Sigrid's face looks almost as if it's frozen, she's standing quietly beside a bed and looking down at her thighs and the floor. The room is full of light and silence, and the wooden floor is made from wide, polished boards, and the windows are high and bright, and outside the window stand some trees with white crowns, silently swaying gently in the wind, and because they are swaying without us being able to hear it—we only see the snow being shaken off—they seem somehow extra quiet, almost mute. And the bed linen is white, and there's nothing else in the room apart from the bed. And Sigrid; Sigrid, who is standing naked and almost immobilized, looking down at her thighs and the floor. On the floor beneath her is a drop of blood, then another appears, then a third drop, big drops of blood that splash onto the wooden boards, perfect drop shapes that explode on the floor. They're so big. And there's blood running down the insides of her thighs, a thick trail of red blood. Shit, Sigrid thinks. Is there nothing here she can wipe it up with? She almost doesn't dare to move, in case she bleeds all over the floor, but she can't just stand here either, so she tries to wiggle over to her rucksack, which is also in the room, though we forgot to mention it. She clamps her legs together and wiggles over so the blood won't be able to drip onto the floor. She rummages around for some underwear and rubs them down her thigh like a cloth, then cleans herself as best she can; she stuffs these briefs inside another pair, which she now pulls on. Then she takes a third pair and cleans the floor. But she'll still have to wash it! Breakfast! Kåre shouts from the kitchen.

•

Breakfast, yes. A meal that's so simple if only one doesn't think about it. Slices of bread with jam or cheese that can be popped in one's mouth, with coffee or tea or milk or juice. A delightfully easy meal, when one hasn't just started one's period and bled all over the floor belonging to the man one came to visit only yesterday, an author whose portrait one has stroked, whom one bumped into by accident by a railing at a lookout point with a view of Laksevåg, and whom one then talked to on the phone for a month, and late in the evening whispered into the receiver, out of the blue, on impulse, "I love you," then waited for a response that never came as one looked at the white walls and ceiling over one's bed, and decided to interpret the reply, "Oh," as a positive answer.

•

Yes, Sigrid calls back, I'll be right there!

•

Breakfast. The meal that, for the past three years, Kåre has usually eaten with Wanda and that he is now going to eat with Sigrid. He's standing stirring the scrambled eggs, which he doesn't notice are crackling at the bottom of the pan, thinking about Wanda. Sigrid appears in the doorway and, red-faced, asks if he has a bucket. Kåre notices that he's burning the scrambled eggs and says fuck, now I'm burning the scrambled eggs, he pulls the pan off the plate and gets a bucket out from under the sink. Are you going to clean? he asks. Don't ask, Sigrid says, and disappears into the bathroom.

•

Wanda, Kåre thinks. If it wasn't over before, it's certainly over now, now that he's had sex with Sigrid, good sex, if he says so himself, he smiles at the scrambled eggs, but he feels the need to cry building in his chest, and suddenly the tears just pour out. Wanda.

•

God, what a name, he said the first time they met, and she laughed, what about Kåre, then, no one is called *Kåre*. Well, there are even fewer people called Wanda, Kåre retorted, and Wanda said: that makes two of us, then. None, and fewer than none. Cheers.

•

She could drink, she certainly could, and so could he. They drank each other under the table that first night, and when they were thrown out and staggered home, they sang *Kåååååre, Waaaaaanda, Kåååååre, Waaaaaanda*, as though they were calling themselves in to dinner. Do you know what, Wanda suddenly said in some park or another, when we say *Kåre* first and then *Wanda*, and say it very fast, it's almost like we're saying *Rwanda*? Something that made them laugh hysterically, they laughed until they collapsed, they had to sit down, we'll be a disaster, Kåre said, and kissed her, for the first time, but in a good way, Wanda said, and then they laughed some more, kissed and laughed, all the way home, here.

•

I can't find the floor cleaner, Sigrid says. She has, however, found—but doesn't mention—a row of skin products that must be Wanda's, in the cupboard under the sink. She looks at Kåre, who is standing there crying. What is it? she asks, and goes over to him and puts her arms around him. It's nothing, Kåre says. I don't really believe you, Sigrid says. Ah well, says Kåre.

3

Dear Sofia Coppola,

This question I wanted to ask you earlier about surfaces: I want to rephrase it. What I would like to ask you is this: What do you do when you're in a grown man's kitchen and he's crying his heart out over some eggs and you're having a hard time trying to understand what's happened, why he's crying, and you think that it might be because he's thinking of his ex-girlfriend whose existence you just discovered when you were looking for some soap in the bathroom cupboard to wash away the blood you bled on his floor earlier on because you suddenly got your period getting out of bed, his ex-girlfriend who's left her expensive creams and makeup there, as some kind of promise, as if she never left? As if she's going to turn up any second and start to rub her face with moisturizing cream with a hint of apricot?

4

Breakfast. Hardly the time to tell him about her dream, to brighten the atmosphere, that she dreamed she was on a strange trip to a cabin with lots of people, a cabin that just got bigger and bigger until it was almost factory-sized, and there were no beds left. So she had to make herself a bed of cushions from the sofa, had to build herself a mattress of different-shaped and stuffed cushions on the floor. That she then went to look for a fitted sheet that would hold them all together, but when she got back, fitted sheet in hand, all the cushions had moved, had spread apart. That she put down the fitted sheet, rearranged the cushions, and when she was going to put the fitted sheet over, the sheet was no longer there. That she thought: oh well, she'd just have to go and get another one! But then when she came back, the cushions had become small plastic containers of take-out rice, and she thought, in desperation, that there was hardly enough there to make a whole mattress, even though it was no doubt fine to lie on soft rice! And that she started to arrange the rice containers into a mattress, and that while she was doing that, it struck her that she was now making a mini-mattress, which, according to the logic of the previous mattress experience, would change, when she went to get a new sheet (because the sheet she had now would certainly disappear), into a normal-sized mattress by the time she got back. That she was happy and optimistic, and really threw herself into arranging the containers of rice. And then she woke up, and it was morning, and she lay there for a while looking out the large, light windows with the trees outside and thought: this is a perfect illustration of deconstruction and its constantly evasive truths! And that she had to laugh because the picture of Paul de Man, one of the fathers of deconstruction, which she had on the wall at home, had thus followed her into her dreams. And she was delighted because the dream was also a perfect illustration of how she herself functioned: she always tried to make things fit, both as a reader of literature and as a person who sought out the company of others, and she always failed. The "cushions" always slid apart, and the "fitted sheet" always disappeared. But this time she'd had the feeling that things would work out. Here, in Kåre's bedroom, she'd had an optimistic dream. So she had basically been happy and optimistic when she got out of bed—before the blood splashed onto the floor without warning, she'd been full of the optimistic feeling from the dream, the feeling that the plastic containers of take-out rice *would transform into a mattress*, and she had woken *in the belief* that everything would be fine, that everything would work out, this, them, her and Kåre, would transform into a mattress! But she tells him about all of this just the same, because she feels that he perhaps needs to hear that she believes in this, she wants this, she wants to sit here at the breakfast table and see his dark face, that's what she wants. She tells him about her dream. Kåre laughs when she says that *we'll transform into a mattress*, just you wait and see! You're too good to be true, he says, giving her cheek a paternal stroke. And then he starts to cry again. The question is, what's holding you back? he says as he cries, and tries to laugh because he's quoting that stupid golf book, but throws out his arms and repeats, as though these words help him to understand the answer to life's great mystery, the origins of the universe, and at the same time, how tragic this answer is: The question is, what's holding you back? What he of course means, but doesn't say out loud, because he's crying, is: Why doesn't he just throw himself into a relationship with this young girl, why is Wanda the one he's thinking about? Wanda with her angry face and sharp bangs? And Sigrid thinks optimistically that when she reads the poem she wrote on a piece of paper that's lying folded in her jacket pocket, a poem that says that her life has been like drifting on the Arctic Ocean, that her ship has been frozen in desolation, but that now, having found Kåre, there is hope that she'll make it, he'll *feel* it, he'll *understand* it, he'll have no doubts. What's holding you ba-ha-hack, Kåre sobs, and his tears have now spilled over into a more fundamental existential despair.

5

Trine is still sitting in bed in a hotel room in Oslo on the January day that Sigrid meets Kåre, and thinks: How can you explain to someone who has never given birth to a child the moment when you give birth to a child? How your vagina is stretched and pulled so much that the skin burns with every thrust the enormous baby's head makes down the canal, like when you force your brain to tackle a thought you can't quite comprehend (for example, the banal but terrible question: What is *outside* the universe, the enormous, incomprehensible, endless universe, with all the stars, all the galaxies, solar systems, planets, all the nebulae, the fantastic Horsehead Nebula that actually *looks like a kind of horse head*, with the head turned away, in a kind of pink mist bedecked with glittering stars, which simply exists, out there in the universe, for all eternity, and resembles a horse on an eternal plain, where does it end, what's beyond it, it *burns* in your brain!), that you can't push because you're scared you'll shit, that you feel someone wiping your ass and you despair: Am I shitting? Then I refuse to push! And then the contractions come, regardless, in enormous paroxysms, and want to turn your rectum inside out in such a way that your arms, head, stomach, spine are helplessly sucked into your body, into the rectum, and how they then in regular shudders come *out* of the rectum (hands, head, fumbling blindly out of your rectum) along with the shit that you shat against your will, and how in a way, you press yourself out of your own rectum while the baby is being pushed out of the birth canal. And then that moment when the baby is suddenly released from your body and everything just pours out of you and you're a broken dam and you see a screaming baby, way down there, all gray over a blue body, wriggling and screaming, and you will always remember it, exactly the way she was lifted up, what her body was like, the small arms trembling with rage, legs pulled up, not her, and not you, but a doll that's come out of another doll, the smallest babushka from the next smallest babushka, the last link in the human race for precisely one hundredth of a second. How to *convey* that? Trine thinks, and looks at her feet, they've nearly turned blue, her feet are so cold. And then, she thinks, what you're thinking is: they can take her away now. That you're done in, that you can't take any more. All you want to do is cry. And turn your head away, for all eternity.

•

Until someone comes and puts a baby in your bed and the baby attaches itself to your breast. Not like a leech, not like a parasite, but like a small, warm baby with an even smaller mouth that tries to suck on your nipple, with arms that move every now and then as though they were underwater, only someone's emptied out all the water.

•

She thinks how intensely she would have hated it if, in that situation—with the baby at her breast—she'd thought: "And you suddenly realize that you really do have something concrete to contribute: milk." And yet she did just that, thought it all the same, just a little bit. She did. She, who normally only had art to give, or something from the borderlands between life and art, now really did have something to give: milk. She hates herself intensely in this moment, but at the same time is terrified and picks up the phone and calls her mother: Is everything okay? Everything's fine, her mother says. Is she taking the bottle all right today? Trine asks. She's taking the bottle fine! her mother says. I'll try to get an earlier plane, Trine says. There's no need, her mother says. No, no, Trine says, and looks out the window, and tries to hold back the shout and the sobs, the shout that fills her, that we can really only call the call home, *the call home*, in other words, Trine wants to go home, she wants to go home to Haldis! Oh, Trine, you're just like a mommy polar bear, aren't you? As you sit here having fallen so completely into your own trap? A mother polar bear on an endless white sheet of ice, howling with fear because she can't see her cubs anywhere on the frozen waste? Yes. But Trine can't give voice to this howl, and certainly not on the phone with her mom, so she coughs and says: let's see how things go. Yes, her mother says, since this is the answer she expected—she has, after all, gotten used to having a daughter who does exactly as she pleases.

•

And then Trine gets up from the bed and turns on the TV. She milks her overfull breasts into the sink, takes a shower, and packs as she thinks about what her next project will be:

to create a visual space with three pink Horsehead Nebulae with three bluish-gray babies dangling from the end of umbilical cords coming out of the eye of each horse head. And three walruses diving through the mist, but only their underbellies will be visible. And underneath it'll say: "This Is Not the Milky Way." She laughs as she hangs her dressing gown up on the hook in the bathroom. Just as she's about to pull on her socks, she stops and looks at her feet. The shape of her big toe on the floor, times two. It looks like a heart. So here she is: two feet in a heart.

6

Robert also looks down at his feet, he's sitting in the Winter
Garden at the Glyptotek, looking down at his feet; he's wearing the new shoes that he bought because he felt he needed
some new shoes for his trip to Copenhagen with Linnea, and
he's feeling—in the second that he looks down at his shoes, a
fifty-one-year-old man sitting under some palms that stretch
up for yards under the glass-domed ceiling—a little sad.
He doesn't know why, or, that is to say, he knows perfectly
well why, he has the distinct feeling that Linnea actually
didn't want him with her, that she led him eagerly into the
Winter Garden and said it was so "utterly delightful to sit
here," bought him a cup of coffee and gave him the brochure
she got when they bought the tickets, said there was no point
in him coming with her, as she was just going to find the
mummy room and she'd be back once she'd had a look around.
So when he now looks down at his new shoes, it's as though
they're a symbol of defeat; black leather shoes, Italian, a bit
tight on top, they're expensive and go perfectly with the suit

and blue shirt that he's wearing, and the expensive watch on his wrist, and Robert of course doesn't know that there's always something oddly mismatched about the way he dresses, as though clothing that should go well together somehow collapses on his body, bulging and twisting in the wrong ways, as is the case right now as he sits under the palms in the Winter Garden, with the vague feeling that something isn't quite as he thinks it is.

•

Linnea doesn't want to go to the Egyptian Collection quite yet, she doesn't dare, so instead of going left into the Egyptian Collection, she goes right, into the Greek Collection. She wanders through the displays of vases, small fired-clay statues and great marble statues of gods, she wanders through the Greek artists' pioneering work in portraying the human body (especially the male body) in 700 BC, having been influenced by the Egyptians, who made the first stylized drawings of people a few hundred years earlier, for example on their coffins, and she visualizes Göran's body, she visualizes Göran's face, Göran's hair and beard, Göran's mouth in the middle of that beard telling her all this, through all the rooms, going on to speak about the Greek city-states and holistic structures and the epoch of harmonious culture; Linnea is so nervous that he might be standing somewhere among the statues, that he might come up behind her, put his arms around her, and say "there you are," as she's imagined in her many fantasies about this meeting two years later, which is now, that she feels dizzy. All of a sudden, there's no way back, he has to be here, it's now, Linnea thinks, or never. The meaning of "now or never" has never been clearer to her, though the "never" in particular makes her feel sick. There's a noise behind her, she turns, but all she sees is a group of American tourists in white sneakers coming into the room, she turns back and hurries on, through rooms of Greco-Roman portraits, small black heads that stare at her, through rooms of ancient Oriental art, and before she knows it, she's there, in the Egyptian Collection.

•

In the meantime, Robert has read the brochure and drunk his coffee, and tried to cheer up, but then he starts to think about the scene in the mummy room and the intense but unfulfilled attraction that is sparked there between "her" and "him" in the screenplay, while "he" talks about how the Egyptians divided the soul into five elements, and all "she" can think is that she wants "him" to grab her around the waist and kiss her. And he ponders on how such an intense attraction can arise out of nothing, how a person can come into a room, and someone else is already there, and then these two people for some reason or another feel that they have to interact in some way, physically. And how it is that a person can come into another person's office, with a manuscript, and the one person immediately feels that he or she is somehow connected to the other, but the other perhaps doesn't feel that they need to interact with the first person at all. Why doesn't the same thing happen for everyone, Robert sits and wonders, somewhat vaguely, to be honest, but we feel we should mention it all the same. And that he looks up at the glass dome and sees the palms stretching up far above him, the green against the light coming in through the glass, and that it makes him dizzy.

7

And here we see Sigrid lying with her back to us, a gray sweater on top of her white vest, on a white bed, in a room with bright windows and a tree in the background outside. The shot is of her lower back, down to her calves, her head and feet aren't visible, and her butt is in the middle, and the butt is wearing pale pink, see-through panties, and her legs are bare. Her body is just lying there, resting, and one can see her buttocks quite clearly, but there's nothing sexual about it, just aesthetic, quiet, waiting. And then, above her buttocks, accompanied by some tranquil music, the first part of a title slowly appears in pale white: "Wait," and then a little farther along, above her hipbone, the rest: "Blink." The picture of Sigrid then gradually fades, and the last word, "Blink," comes gliding toward us and remains there in the dark and is crystal clear for a few seconds before the title and picture fade out completely.

8

But really. What happens is that out of Sigrid's butt, out from among the black hairs that grow around her anus, comes something we can't quite identify at first, it's small, thin, and unclear, but then it moves, it wriggles, wriggles farther and farther out of her bottom, and eventually turns out to be a butterfly, in glorious, glittering colors. It stops, just outside her ass, beats its wings, as though checking to see that they work, perhaps, before flying off, and then we discover that there's an almost transparent silk banner tied to it that's pulled out of Sigrid's behind as it flaps away, which says: I'M PRETENDING TO HANDLE THIS.

9

In other words, this: being in Kåre's house with Wanda's skin care products in the cupboard under the sink, and Kåre, who just keeps crying and crying. She says to him that maybe he should go and lie down for a bit, sleep, maybe that will help? He gives her a hug and says yes, it might. He's going to go and lie down, and sleep for a while. Are you sure that's okay, will you be all right on your own for a couple of hours? Kåre asks. Yes, of course, Sigrid says. Kåre kisses her on the forehead with dry, hard lips and then leaves her, and the way in which he strokes her shoulders, and the fact that he's walking away from her as he does it, gives her the feeling that this won't work, that it's over. What should she do? Should she just pack her bag and leave?

•

She walks around his flat as quietly as she can. She looks at the bookshelves, which are long, with double rows of books. She tries to see which ones have worn spines, which ones he's taken out time and time again, she smells them, they smell sweet, possibly of tobacco, she opens some of the books, the paper is coarse against her fingers, the ink of each letter pressed into the paper, these are old books, Sigrid thinks, and reflects on the fact that she's now looking at something that he's looked at, something that's meant something to him, but she can't grasp it, she just smells the sweet smell of the paper and feels slightly sick. She's trying, she thinks with corners of her mouth turned down because she's feeling sick, to break through and grasp something that is essentially him, but instead feels sick! These books make her feel sick, the smell makes her feel sick. She *understands* what that means: that deep down, she isn't one hundred percent sure that this is one hundred percent right. That she has to convince herself that it is, certainly when he suddenly bursts out crying and seems to be very unsure as well. She thinks about his card with the wooden chair on the front and feels reassured.

•

She'll sit down. She'll sit down on one of his chairs and think, like a secret message to herself, that now *she has sat down*, that's what she's done. Beloved are those who sit down. There's not a lot of furniture in the living room, and most of it is dark wood with smooth leather, but it's exactly how she wants to live when she grows up: simple, light, and peaceful. A bit worn, shabby, but clean, simple. Wide wooden floorboards. And an old black lacquered rococo table by the window with a glass vase with a single stem of pink lilies; they look like grotesque mouths, she thinks, each with five protruding tongues. She sits down on the dark leather chair (now *she is sitting down*) by the rococo table, she feels the cool leather against the backs of her thighs.

10

And what is Sigrid wearing, when she sits down on one of Kåre's chairs? Answer: an oversized, checked flannel pajama top. Kåre was wearing the bottoms, and she the top, that was what he wanted, yesterday, that she should put it on, he'd bought the pajamas because she was coming, he laughed, pajamas and lilies, that's what he'd bought, and he'd thought that was fantastic as he walked home with the two items, because Sigrid was coming. Pajamas and lilies. Him in the bottoms, her in the top. So she couldn't exactly refuse, she couldn't say that wearing an oversized man's shirt was a cliché in her opinion, a typical expression of male aesthetics, male perception, a perception that specifically objectivized women, he would make her into a cliché by doing that—making her pad around being fragile and vulnerable in an oversized top and thus live up to all the myths—and, not least, by complying she would thereby undermine her own intellect and capacity for criticizing metaphors, wouldn't she? She realized it was impossible to say all this. And then he

sang the whole deLillos song "Cool in Pajamas" as they
stood brushing their teeth in front of the mirror, and she
couldn't help but be impressed that he was like that, so natural. And it made her not a little happy, because she was *chang-
ing* something, she was now on her way to becoming someone
else, someone who actually *dressed* herself in the aforemen-
tioned pajama top: it was the end of the line for her old, ana-
lytical mind, now she was just going to pad around in a
pajama top and *live*. Have sex. Drink wine. No, whiskey actually. Or gin.

•

But then: smell some books and feel nauseous. She looks at
the only small picture hanging on the walls, a murky painting of a boathouse in somber colors. Not exactly Van Gogh's
sunflowers, or a photocopy of Paul de Man from a textbook,
but an original painting. Art should cost something, Kåre
had said, if you're going to have something on the walls, it
should be expensive. Art should *mean* something, not be
reproduced. Don't just hang something up for the sake of
having something on the walls, like Van Gogh's sunflowers
because they're nice and yellow, sort of thing. Sigrid had
blushed. Yes, but, Sigrid had said, it's possible that Van Gogh's
sunflowers actually mean something to someone, even if
they're hanging in thousands of homes as cheap reproduc-
tions. I bet you it's millions, Kåre said, so Sigrid said, I've got
a reproduction of the sunflowers on my wall. She didn't like
him much right then, it didn't fit with what she thought he
was. Kåre looked at her and laughed. Well, he said, at least
it's not Monet's water lilies! He ruffled her hair. Van Gogh's
sunflowers, eh? he said. Of course they may mean something

to someone, Kåre said, it's not that, for me it's also about showing solidarity with artists. I would rather use my money to support a living artist than give it to an already lucrative high-turnover industry that spews out cheap and cheerful copies of cutesy art. Sigrid's mouth was dry. Not everyone, she said, can afford to support living artists, and just because lots of people like something it doesn't necessarily mean it's fluffy. It *is* so fluffy, Kåre said, and looked at her, he thought this was amusing, finally she had to fight for something, you can't deny it. In which case, I don't care, Sigrid said, and felt her heart pounding in her throat. Hooray, Kåre said and laughed, and gave her a hug, but she was shaking all over and didn't want him to feel it, he held her close and said that he was proud of her, she'd actually said what she thought.

•

A bit of heat, Kåre had once said on the phone, that's what he needed. Dynamism, being alive. They'd certainly had *that*, he and Wanda! he said in a warm, shiny voice, and Sigrid thought it was more due to the whiskey than the love and a longing for the heat that he and Wanda had had. You could argue loudly, for all he cared, in fact, preferably shout at each other, as long as you stood up for what you believed in. Sigrid wasn't very good at screaming and shouting and felt slightly uncomfortable when he said this. Of course, she had said, and looked away, before she'd had time to use the trick Jens Stoltenberg used when he was prime minister: to stare at precisely what you wanted to look away from when there was a danger you might look away. One should be oneself, one should be genuine and natural, and Sigrid was just that, he thought, even though she was a little more careful than he might like. But thus far, when he had intellectualized the two relationships, the one with Wanda versus the one with Sigrid (against his own better judgment, of course, as he would rather not intellectualize things at all), he'd come to the conclusion that with him and Wanda, the ruling principle was that of *the individual*, whereas with Sigrid, it was more *the collective*. He saw the collective in her, unity, something one didn't need to imagine, one didn't need to be like this or that, one could just be oneself and breathe freely, calmly, that's what she had, Kåre had thought when he thought about her in those quiet hours by the window in the flat where Sigrid is now sitting with her head on the table, there was something very natural and uncomplicated about her, about her hair, which wasn't dyed, like Wanda's, Sigrid's hair was somehow honest, he thought, and he had to smile, because that's how it should be. Wanda's hair: thin and black, Wanda's eyes: ominously black-lined. Wanda's mouth: red. All of Wanda: thin and dressed in leather. Wanda: the bassist. Wanda, over him with her strong, naked body and eyes hidden behind her thin black hair.

•

But, Sigrid had said on the phone, what if being careful is part of being natural? If shouting and screaming is not the way one does things? Her mouth had been a little dry. Then you have to change it, Kåre said. It's like hiding yourself, not being true to yourself. But that's what I'm like, Sigrid thought. Does that mean I'm not genuine? She felt a bit contemptuous of his argument, but could she express it? No.

•

But one can't agree on everything, Sigrid thinks, where she's sitting with her head on the black lacquer table, it's not possible, she thinks, for two people to live together for their whole lives and to be the people they *are*. It's only natural to feel a little contempt every now and then. Because, after all, that's what they're going to do, live a whole life together. They've talked a lot about it on the phone. Doors have opened since they met, doors they didn't know existed, neither she, lonely and downcast as *she* is, nor he, distant and cold as *he* is—Kåre has even thought, in those quiet hours by the window, that Sigrid is the light, salvation, a bit like Jesus for him. He's also imagined (but he hasn't said a word about this) Sigrid sitting, soft and slender, with a small, sleeping baby in her arms. Her hair is falling softly along her jaw, and she has a very maternal expression on her face as she looks down, smiling, at the tiny baby face. Children? Is that what's going to happen now? Kåre has thought, because he never had this fantasy about Wanda, or anyone else, so it must mean something. So: doors have opened for them, and they're about to go through these doors that have opened, and stay there, Sigrid thinks. She sees a crystal whiskey decanter standing on an old corner cupboard, it must be the one he poured his drinks from while he was talking to her in the evenings this past month, when his voice took on a warmer, shinier tone the more he's drunk, and she didn't like it, she really *didn't* like it, but she's told herself she has to stop being so childish, people drink, *get over it*, she's told herself, and insisted that it's part of normal life, the normal life she's now going to become part of too.

•

So there was *that*, a little contempt, but there was also a little of something that felt like love, like yesterday, when he played PJ Harvey for her, from the *new* record, as he said, as though he was performing a sacred rite or something (and it was, for Kåre, who hadn't really listened to PJ Harvey's new record, he somehow got stuck on *Stories from the City, Stories from the Sea*, where she sings the line about touching someone's head, but now, he felt, it was time, with Sigrid and the new era he was entering, to listen to PJ Harvey's *new* record, *White Chalk*), and Sigrid watched Kåre's face as Harvey sang the beautiful, but slightly ominous, words "Dear darkness, won't you cover, cover me again?" PJ Harvey sang in such a reedy voice over the very delicate and beautiful piano accompaniment, with a few heavy beats on the deeper notes, a kind of soft, rolling waltz, and it was as though Kåre's face fused with the music and lyrics, imagine listening like that, Sigrid thought, and felt a sudden love for this listening face, she wanted to be close to it, say that she loved it, touch it, or best of all, *be* the voice and the piano, and the lyrics, and fill the whole room like a soft, rolling waltz—obviously not knowing that if she had been this, in her romantic, cosmic fantasy (the voice and the piano and the lyrics, this song), she would have been something that told Kåre something that he, as we already know, had tried to hide: "Dear darkness, won't you cover, cover me again?" and that would have had the *opposite* effect on Kåre from what she imagined, she would then, personally, have had exactly the same effect on Kåre as the song did yesterday, when he stood listening to it, with Sigrid standing beside him: he'd had the slightly alarming feeling that Sigrid, potentially the mother of his future children, was like a piece of furniture or a cushion or something else one's bought in the belief that it would be perfect for the flat, that this piece of furniture would so perfectly

reflect something in oneself in terms of aesthetics and iden-
tity, but then somehow sticks out when it's in place, and one
doesn't quite know what to do with it. Where to put it. And
it was expensive. Dear darkness. Come, won't you cover,
cover me again? echoed a voice in the depths of Kåre.

•

Sigrid feels a little cold. She's taken the fact that she's not
dressed yet as a sign that her new, adult, and carefree existence has started, but now this existence means that her feet
are cold. She looks over at the sofa, there's a blanket lying
there. She'll go over and sit on the sofa and wrap the blanket
around her, as if she were at home. The blanket prickles
against her legs, but it'll soon warm up, she thinks, now she's
going to sit on this sofa and try to recapture the feeling she
had last night when she couldn't sleep, lying naked under
the duvet and looking around the room and listening to
Kåre breathing: there were no curtains over the windows, so
she could look right up to the stars, and the room was night-
black and cold and unfamiliar, and she felt unfamiliar, the
unfamiliar feeling of the duvet, the pillow, the mattress,
the man, the breathing, the room, until suddenly she noticed, looking out the window, up at the sky, that the Big
Dipper was out there twinkling. There was a pressure in her
chest; it was a little ridiculous, unfortunately, how seriously
she took signs like that: Was it real, she wondered, or, to be
more precise, experienced, since she didn't actually *formulate*
this overwhelming feeling to herself using the words "is it
real," no, that's just our own inadequate and almost self-
consciously unsuccessful—but thus ironically successful—
attempt to convey what she felt, that it was *the Big Dipper* of all

things that was twinkling at her from the sky and seemed to know that she was lying there small and alone in a stranger's bed, and came to her now, when everything was utterly unfamiliar, as a sign, a sign that she was, in fact, *at home?* It made her think about the girl they'd managed to find in the forest because she'd used the light on her mobile phone, she'd gotten lost, and she didn't have enough credit left to call anyone, but she still had a little battery power, enough to light up the display screen on her phone, and because she was calm, she managed to wait until late at night when a helicopter finally circled near to where she was lying and she blinked at it with her phone. Imagine, Sigrid thought. Wait, blink, survive. And then she looked up at the stars. And that's what you've done too, she thought all at once, a sudden revelation as to the inner being of stars, and this sudden insight and symbolism made her feel warm all over, you have waited, blinked, survived! How long does a star live? she thought, they don't live forever, but they've certainly twinkled for as long as *she*'s been alive! And, thought Sigrid—and looked over at Kåre's neck, seeing how the night sort of held him in its embrace, like a thin son, Sigrid thought, and thought that she should make a note of all this on her mobile phone, only the phone was down in the kitchen, and she watched his shoulder rise and fall with his breathing—and she thought, that's what I've done too, I've shone and shone and finally someone has seen me twinkling, and now I'm going to survive. And now she was *completely* overwhelmed, and the tears ran from her eyes, and down her nose and throat under the duvet. When she'd finished crying, she lay there and looked at Kåre. Here he was, in real life, the man from the author's photograph. He had such defined features, he almost looked a bit frightening in his sleep, his skin was so smooth in the dark, he was almost like a statue. What if she were to snuggle up against him, surely she could do that, and maybe she would fall asleep then. She edged her way closer and when she moved her head to look at him one last time before she lay down to sleep, her hair stroked his chin, and Kåre started and sat up with a noise that sounded like an animal living a wild life in the forest, which had now been caught; Kåre looked at her with wild eyes and he gasped for breath, what, he said, eh, he said, and rubbed his face, oh God, he said, it's you, it's you, and then he fell back again and straight to sleep. Sigrid didn't know how to interpret that, and hadn't dared ask him this morning, and when she thinks about it now, on the sofa, she almost laughs, she must ask him about it when he wakes up.

·

She wishes she could automatically feel a bit more at home here. She tries to lean back against the sofa, because she realizes she hasn't relaxed at all, her shoulders are tense, she tries to relax her shoulders against the back of the sofa, but doesn't quite manage. It's so quiet. Only the hum of the fridge from the kitchen, not a sound from upstairs.

·

Her phone rings. Oh no, Kåre will wake up! She jumps up and runs to her jacket that's hanging out in the hall, it's Magnus, she hasn't spoken to him for a month, not since she called and said that she just couldn't write the article about the women in those oversized men's shirts, hello, she whispers into the phone; hello? Magnus says, and she feels the urge to shush him, he's talking so loudly, but she just whispers hello back and hurries into the bathroom and shuts the door as quietly as she can. What's wrong? Magnus says. I have to be quiet, Sigrid says. Someone's sleeping, she says. Aha, Magnus says in a teasing voice. Yes, yes, Sigrid says. I wondered how you were getting on, but I guess you're fine then, Magnus says, I won't keep you. No, no, it's fine, Sigrid says, but maybe we should speak another time, when I don't need to be so quiet. Yes, of course, Magnus says, but then suddenly she doesn't want him to go, she felt safe hearing his voice, she can't get her words out, she closes her eyes and lips so she doesn't release the sobs that are suddenly forcing their way up her throat. Sigrid? Magnus says, are you there? Did you hang up? But she can't make a sound, because if she makes the slightest sound now, it will be the sound of crying, so she says nothing, hello, Magnus says, hello, hello, Sigrid, I'm going to put the phone down, maybe the line's gone down, if you can hear me, I'll give you a ring in a couple of days. Bye, he says, and then he hangs up. Sigrid sits down on the toilet seat with her hand in front of her mouth.

11

Here we see Sigrid as she comes out of the bathroom in the oversized pajama top with a slightly reinvigorated spirit. She could bake some buns, she thinks. Buns are soft and warm, and food always helps, in any situation. But she doesn't know his kitchen, and the first thing she has to do is find out if he has yeast, and flour, and butter, and sugar, and milk. She tiptoes into the kitchen and starts to open cupboard after cupboard, as quietly as she can. She discovers a special technique for opening them quietly, and closing them almost all the way before letting them shut themselves properly, and when she takes down the bag of flour, she does it slowly so the paper doesn't rustle. The doorbell rings, but there's not a sound from the loft. She thinks it would be worse if whoever it was rang again than if she answered the door and revealed her presence, even though it might be Wanda—in which case she could get her skin care products from the bathroom, put them in a plastic bag, and give them to her, face expressionless—so she tiptoes out to the front door. It's a man. Is Kåre not home?

he asks, and puts something he was holding in his hand back in the inside pocket of his jacket. He's asleep, Sigrid says. The man looks annoyed. They must have made some arrangement, Sigrid thinks. Okay, I can come back later. Can I give him a message? Sigrid asks. Who are you, by the way? the man asks. I'm Sigrid, Sigrid says. We've just, Sigrid starts, and the man laughs, I can see. No! Sigrid says, we've just started seeing each other, she says. Tell him that Ståle came by, and that I'll come back around five, he says. Okay, Sigrid says with a smile, but Ståle has already turned around and is on his way down the stairs. Ståle, she writes on a scrap of paper, five o'clock. And then puts it on the kitchen table.

•

She wants to make buns, but realizes that it involves a lot of sounds that might wake Kåre; the flour bag *will* rustle, the bowls *will* clatter. She'll have to wait awhile. She can read the newspaper. She moves the note and opens the paper, but the pages rustle so loudly; she tries to turn them as quietly as she can, and winds up reading a lot of stuff she's not particularly interested in, because turning the pages quietly takes such effort that she tries to stick to one page. Then suddenly she hears Kåre coming down the stairs to the kitchen. He stands there and looks at her. You *can* make some noise even if I'm asleep, he says. I didn't want to disturb you, she says. I hate the fact that you restrict yourself because of me, he says. Please stop doing that, Kåre says, and stares at her, and she sees something hard in his face that makes her feel even more insecure, she gets the same statue feeling that she had last night, it's cold, alien. Just be yourself! he says. Yes, she says, and feels an iron band closing around her chest because she *has* been herself, she's only been as quiet as she always is when someone is sleeping nearby, it presses tighter and tighter around her chest, and eventually she starts to cry, and the butterfly rubs away what was written on the silk banner, and writes a new message, which says: THUS I GO TO PIECES COMPLETELY! And then adds: I AM FALLING TO BITS, IMPOSSIBLE FOR THE HUMAN EAR TO HEAR (THE LOUDEST THING IT COULD SOUND LIKE WOULD BE THE SOUND OF SUGAR FALLING).

12

Apropos of falling to pieces: one morning in the life of the Belgian literary theorist Paul de Man, when he was a child, he stood looking at a stone and watched it sink into wet black mud. It sank slowly, and Paul de Man stood watching it for several hours, until the stone was swallowed completely, the mud enveloping the stone more and more, until the dry gray surface of the stone was covered by more and more wet black mud until there was only a tiny spot left, and how the wet black mud became whole again, over and around the stone, closed in on itself again after the stone had materialized there and made its surface imperfect. Paul de Man had stood there for several hours, and even though he was only a child, he reflected on the fact that that is what happens when we sleep. That's what it's like when we dream. We sink into wet black mud. And no one can see us. And no one knows where we are. And no one can tell from our perfect surface that we're hiding a stone. And then he noticed he was hungry and dizzy.

•

Here we see Paul de Man, a good many years later. He's sitting in his office, there are lots of books in the background. His stomach is impressively rotund. He's wearing a suit and tie—and in profile, we would be able to see that his tie, shirt, and suit curve over his body and round stomach in a fine arch. His eyes are closed, light streams in through the window, the light is filtered through the leaves on the maple trees that are being blown by the wind, so his face appears dappled. Under the dappled light, Paul de Man's face is as unmoving as a stone. The names Sigrid and Kåre are written on the board behind him, to the left of the bookshelves, and under Sigrid there's a column of other names, but under Kåre, there's nothing, just one word: nothing. But our focus is drawn back to Paul de Man, it's impossible to focus on the board, we try to force our attention back, but the focus *is* Paul de Man!

•

And this: when Paul de Man was little, he often felt like he was drowning. He could be sitting perfectly still on the edge of a sofa in Antwerp, with a cup of tea in front of him, surrounded by his family, and suddenly get the feeling that he was drowning. It was as if he was sinking into himself and couldn't breathe. It felt like his nipples were being stabbed with small needles. The stone that had been swallowed by the black, wet mud had stayed in him, and now, on the edge of the sofa, it was as though he himself was such a stone, and he was sinking into his chest, his chest that he felt was black, wet mud from the neck down. He could see it: his own face sinking in the black, wet mud. The tip of his nose sticking up. Then he disappeared. He could hear a sound, which possibly resembled this: *ssupppphhh*. It gave him claustrophobia. He had to get up and leave the room. He had to go to his own room and open the window and look out at all the roofs that lay there in the strange white light of the low November sun, and feel his face slowly, but surely, breaking up.

•

He later started to study engineering. He wanted to build something. But one day, in the middle of finishing some elementary piece of load-bearing structure, he got the feeling he was drowning in his own chest. The prickling in his nipples. He heard the sound: *ssupppphhh*. And he got up and left without saying anything. Then he started chemistry, but later transferred to literature. And it was here that he would find success in life and become a professor. He married a Romanian woman, and had two children with her. He had the feeling that everything was a movement that started, then disappeared. This made him desperate/indifferent.

•

During the Second World War, he wrote a number of articles for pro-Nazi publications, before switching sides and becoming an anti-Nazi, and wanting to leave Belgium, which was governed by collaborators (among others, his own uncle). He took his wife and children with him to the border between France and Spain, and due to some inexplicable mix-up, his wife and children ended up in Argentina and Paul de Man ended up in the United States, where he was given a professorship at a university. He never saw his wife and children again. No one knows why. But we can see Paul de Man's wife and two children quite clearly: three nose tips sticking up. And then: *ssupppphhh.*

•

Paul de Man often sat in his office in the United States and thought about the stone he had seen back then, and how things might have been different if he hadn't seen it; if he, for example, had been distracted by a deer that suddenly appeared at the edge of the forest, if he had looked another way, if he had simply turned around. The big maple trees outside his window were often beautifully lit by sunlight when he thought about this, and the light filtered in through the window and dappled Paul de Man's face.

•

And here is Paul de Man, standing in his office, just like that, with all his books in the background, Paul de Man, who has made many unexpected changes in his life, but who didn't make the one he should perhaps have made, to turn away from the stone that was sinking, and thus perhaps to change the course of his entire life, or, at least, the symbolic framework he has created for himself.

13

If we look closely, we see that Paul de Man in this picture in fact resembles, of all things, the pink Horsehead Nebula that Trine was thinking about earlier. It must be something to do with the fact that he looks so distant, yet so solid and tangible, as he does here in his office in front of all the books, with his rounded belly, but equally as though he could just disintegrate, evaporate, be sucked up into the universe like some kind of glittering dust and there fall into place and manifest as a distinct nebula, a nebula that we feel we could put our arms around and hug (a feeling that is, of course, nothing more than an illusion).

14

But this distant and tangible Horsehead Nebula quality makes us think, inevitably, of Elida, who is standing on the bridge in Prague right now. It's early in the morning the day after she's drunk a tankard of beer and failed to achieve a feeling of love and harmony with Magnus. Elida stands there and looks down at the river, there's a distance in her eyes and being, then she suddenly thinks of something and turns toward the castle again. It's so early in the morning that no other tourists are out and about, and it's dark, the thick Prague darkness lies pregnant with morning over the town, the odd drink vendor has started to unpack his wares here and there, they don't nod to her as she passes along the bridge, up to the castle, but they do perhaps look up after she's passed, and see a slim girl with sand-colored straight hair, a blue trench coat, and a red leather bag slowly crossing the bridge as though needing to keep an eye on the cobblestones she's walking over.

·

She follows the map and comes to a long set of steps, and smiles to herself when she sees the steps, because of course there has to be a long, long flight of steps up to the castle, steps with yellow stone walls on either side, at just the right height so one can look out over the town. It's dark, but the steps are lit by old-fashioned black iron lamps on the right-hand side, and she looks at the zigzag pattern of light and dark stones on the steps; a lonely tree that stretches its branches over the stone wall makes her feel at one with her surroundings—she is also, she thinks, a lonely tree stretching its branches over a stone wall! And then she sees what couldn't be seen from the bottom of the steps: the narrow opening onto the square in front of the castle is closed by a tall iron gate. And beside the gate stands a guard with a gun or something similar over his shoulder. She goes up to it all the same. The closer she gets, the more the castle looms over her, but it's behind the gate, of course it's behind a gate. She asks the guard, is it open? but the guard doesn't answer, doesn't look at her, she tries again, when does it open? She stands there until he looks at her, she thinks it's idiotic that he can't answer her, there's no one else here! He shakes his head almost imperceptibly. She looks in at the square. In a way, this is how it should be, that she can't get any closer. She goes up to the gate, takes hold of two bars, and pokes her face in between them. In a way it's perfect, she realizes, it really is, that she can't get in. Hello, castle, she thinks. She starts to walk back down and looks out over Prague and all the lights twinkling at her, and the Charles Bridge over there, and the river, and the tram lines on the streets. Dawn breaks.

•

Magnus is still asleep when she slips back into the room, he's lying with his mouth open, and she has to wake him and tell him it's over. But maybe first she'll lie down a little and look up at the ceiling.

15

Yes, says Viggo, I've just opened. Good, says the man, and comes in the door; it's no one he knows. Could I have a coffee to go, please? he asks. Yes, I just need to turn the machine on, Viggo says, I haven't gotten that far yet. That's fine, the man says, I'll sit here and wait. He sits down at the table closest to the counter and takes a newspaper out of his briefcase. Viggo starts when he sees something sticking out from the brief-case, a piece of red wool, a small piece of red wool.

•

The answer to the question we asked earlier, if Viggo has changed over the course of ten years, is twofold: (a) yes, after all, he's running a café, something that would have been un-thinkable ten years ago, and (b) no, he's still knocked for a loop by little things like a piece of red wool. He still gets the feeling sometimes that a box of matches on the table might explode at any moment, and he still gets red in the face, and Josef, his employee, has to lead him over to a chair, plonk him down behind the counter, and ask: Afraid something's going to explode? And Viggo will nod, and Josef will get him a glass of water. Take it easy, man, Josef, whom he's told all about this, will say. It won't hurt you, and then he'll put a hand on his shoulder, it's just a box of matches, okay? And Viggo will smile and drink the water and try to think that this won't explode either, it won't, shards of glass won't rain down on his face along with the water, it will just slide gently out of a solid glass, into his mouth. But Josef won't be there until ten today, and there's a small piece of red wool sticking out from the suited man's briefcase.

•

A girl comes in the door, and *we* immediately recognize her as Elida, but Viggo doesn't, Viggo just notices that he's breathing easier now, because after all, it'll be harder for the man, if he is indeed an enemy, to try anything with someone else in the café. There was a robbery at the kiosk farther down the street a week ago, and Viggo has kept a knife behind the counter ever since. It's not inconceivable for Viggo that armed robbers might be dressed in suits and have leather briefcases and look like an estate agent he's seen before and who has an office on the same street as the café. Elida hangs her jacket on the back of a chair by the window and puts her bag down on the chair beside it, then comes over to the counter. Could I have a cup of tea, please? Elida asks, with milk. Of course, Viggo says, that'll be twenty kroner. The girl looks at him with a strange expression on her face. Perhaps twenty kroner is a bit pricey, perhaps that's what she's thinking, he thinks, and blushes as he puts some tea into a tea ball, he doesn't want it to be an expensive café, but it has to cost something, otherwise it won't work. But the strange expression on Elida's face has nothing to do with the price of tea, but rather with Viggo, whom she recognizes, he hasn't changed that much in ten years, he's just a little older, more distinguished, and he's still the most beautiful man she's seen in all her life. And now he's here, in front of her, the day after she came back from Prague and came to visit her aunt in Bergen, to get away from Oslo and Magnus for a while, to Magnus's deep despair—now things *definitely* won't go well at his audition for the national broadcast orchestra! And suddenly Viggo is standing there and is just as fantastic as she remembers from Anna Mortensen's funeral when they looked into each other's mouth in the basement of the chapel, and just as she remembers him from her dreams, when he kisses, kisses, and kisses her. She blushes from the inside out, and when they look at each other again, when Viggo hands her a steaming tea in a tall glass, they are both equally red in the face: Viggo because he wonders if twenty kroner is too expensive for this girl who he thinks is rather pretty, and Elida because she remembers that she stood in front of him with her tongue out. And when they look into each other's eyes in that flushed moment, it's too much for them both and they both have to look down. (Music for this section of the book: something beautiful.) Elida rummages in her purse for a twenty-kroner coin. Here you go, she says, and puts the coin into his hand without looking at him. Viggo takes the fact that she doesn't look at him when she puts the twenty-kroner coin in his hand as a sign that she really does think it's too expensive. Thank you, he says. Then she looks up at him again, takes the glass of tea and goes back to her table by the window, sits down, takes *The Castle* out of her bag and puts it on the table, wonders if she should tell him who she is. But she doesn't dare! She dips the infuser ball in and out of the tea, watches the man in a suit disappear out the door with a cup in his hand. Damn, she forgot the milk. She can't face going back to the counter, she'll only blush even more. Sorry, I forgot the milk, a voice suddenly says beside her, and a hand pushes a small jug of milk toward her. She looks at him. Thank you, she says. Not at all, he says, and looks at her shyly, he so desperately wants to do something good, to make up for the tea being so expensive. He notices the book on the table, oh, he says, are you reading that, yes, she says. It's my favorite book, Viggo says, and Elida smiles, astonished, is it? Yes. That and Dante's *Divine Comedy*. Really? Elida says. That's my favorite book too. And *The Castle*, of course. Through me [you] pass into eternal pain! Viggo says, and smiles. Eternal, I endure eternally, Elida says, in a deep, theatrical voice: Abandon all hope, ye who enter here. Viggo laughs. That's *incredible*, he says. He has to take a step back, put his hand to his hair, look at the floor, smiling all the while. I'll never forget, Viggo says, in a slightly thick voice, the scene in *The Castle*, where K tries to get to the castle, and struggles through the deep snow with his two useless helpers. He never gets there, does he? Elida nods enthusiastically, as only those who know exactly what the other person is talking about, or quoting, can. And there's another scene I remember, the one where he's been trying to get hold of a man who I think is called Klamm, but doesn't manage, he's at an inn, and K has to hide so he's not discovered, and he lies down in Klamm's carriage, and as he lies there he's sure that his life is over, but that the thin strip of light from the inn, where Klamm is, might lead him to the castle, um, he feels that the thin strip of light from the inn makes life bearable, it's enough. Elida doesn't realize that this is Viggo's great speech to her, she doesn't realize that this is his symbolic speech to her, the speech of someone who has just had the experience he's longed for all his life, that someone else would be like him, think like him, and that she is the small strip of light he has glimpsed from where he's lain in a carriage outside an inn for his entire life—Elida is just very enthusiastic. Do you know what! Elida says, I'm writing my thesis on *precisely* that, the snow in *The Castle*! Viggo looks at her. Really? he says; yes! she says, I'm going to write about how . . .

•

A few hours later. The sign on the door to the café says CLOSED.

•

ELIDA: And there I was, on the bridge in Prague, and I got this peculiar feeling that this was *time*, that everything was frozen and alive at the same time. And the thing is, why am I so obsessed with everything that's frozen? Why is it the frozen lake, in particular, in hell that fascinates me so, why is it always the frozen lake I think about, that it exists in me, when I'm at my most lonely? And why write about *the snow*, in particular, in *The Castle*?

VIGGO: But it's not actually frozen.

ELIDA: No, but it's an obstacle, and it's everywhere.

VIGGO *(strokes Elida on the cheek)*

ELIDA'S INNER SELF *(shines from a point deep inside)*

EVEN HER SAND-COLORED HAIR *(glitters, as though it were tinglingly happy)*

ELIDA: Viggo
VIGGO: Elida
VIGGO AND ELIDA *(kiss)*
ALL THE SNOW IN THE CASTLE *(snows and snows and snows, lightly, floating downward and upward at the same time as Viggo and Elida kiss and kiss and kiss and kiss and kiss)*

•

A good deal of fantastic *kissing later*

•

Viggo looks over at the table where the man in the suit sat and waited for his coffee, and the piece of red wool is lying on the floor, almost flashing, but it *won't explode.* What is it? Elida asks, it's that piece of red wool there, Viggo says, it must have fallen out of that-man-who-was-here-earlier's briefcase. Elida blushes. I, she starts, I know of a red thread between us, actually, other than that we're both fascinated by the snow in *The Castle,* and love Dante's *Divine Comedy,* she says. What's that? Viggo asks, that we speak the same dialect? Because I also noticed that, Viggo says. We met at your grandmother's funeral ten years ago, I don't know if you remember, Elida says. You'd just had a tooth knocked out. Is it you, Viggo says, the girl who let me look in her mouth? Yes, Elida says, but you know what? She takes the gold tooth out of her pocket. My father found this in a salmon four years later. I fell a little in love with you at the funeral, and then when this tooth turned up, I liked to think it was yours. Let me see, Viggo says, and studies the tooth. It's a bit gray, the gold is tarnished. The root's broken. It's impossible to tell if it's my tooth or not, Viggo says, strange. You would have thought you'd recognize your own teeth. Elida laughs and takes the tooth and puts it back in her pocket. We'll just say it's your tooth. She leans forward and kisses him again.

•

And one would wish that everything was like that, always. But then things always slide, out and out! First things slip inward and inward (the rushing feeling of love and understanding), but then gradually things start to slide out again. And when Elida leaves the café and is walking back to her aunt's, her face tender from all the kissing, she thinks that she wishes they could skip that stage. Whereas Viggo stands holding the piece of red wool in his hand and thinks that he *wishes* he wasn't who he was, so that whatever was going to happen wouldn't be affected by the fear that the way he sometimes was, nervous and helpless, would catch up with them and swamp that which was now, suddenly, and was so wonderful, finally. How would she deal with it if he suddenly had to throw up because of a pair of tights, or if he started to sweat buckets because he thought a dust bunny might explode! What if they have children, Viggo thinks. Would *they* also have to suffer this? A father who suddenly, trembling, disappears into a cupboard? Elida, for her part, thinks that in a way she wishes they didn't need to get to know each other better. Then they could avoid him finding out that she wasn't as exciting and interesting as he thought she was, that she could be stupid, frightened, and angry. Not to mention extremely uptight. Which was why she was obsessed with snow and ice. Because she *has*, *has*, and *has* that frozen lake inside her. Oh, she wishes they could never get to the stage where it dawns on him that she has sides other than those he first saw, and where he retreats into himself as he walks along the road, having said goodbye to her in a taxi, for example, because he had to go to work and she was going home, that he reflected on it and realized that she wasn't as smart as he had at first thought, that what she'd said just now in the taxi was far from what he thought himself, and that this showed that she wasn't as much like him as he'd first thought, and that the red thread between them was in fact just a piece of wool that could easily come apart, or like the red threads of flesh that hold loose teeth in place, and which become even longer if one pulls and twists the tooth, and which eventually let go of the tooth forever. She *wishes so much* that they could never get to that point in the taxi where he says goodbye in a slightly awkward way and then closes the door and lets himself into the café and sits down behind the counter and pours himself a little coffee in a cup, while she sits in the taxi and feels perhaps that she's given away too much, that she shouldn't have spoken so fast, so off the top of her head, so self-analytically, "why am I so obsessed with *snow*," ooooh, that she hadn't shown how stupid and self-centered she was, something she's ashamed of. She wishes, at the very least, they were *over* the getting-to-know-each-other stage, done with trembling one moment and reevaluating the next, and that they could move on in the relationship equipped with the new eyes they might then look at the other with, and that the first shock of discovering they were not quite as they first thought had already settled, and that they could meet and be simply *happy* to meet, because the bad sides were livable-with and did not overshadow the good! This is what Elida thinks, with a worried expression on her face as she walks home; she doesn't notice anything of what's going on around her, and all we can do is wish them well, in everything, and hope for the best.

16

Haldis is asleep when Trine goes into her room in the afternoon. Trine tiptoes over to the cot and looks down at the little head lying on the pillow, the tiny, soft features of her face, the small mouth that's the very image of Knut's mouth. Arms up on either side of her head, as though she'd fallen backward, hands balled, but her fingers easily opened again, with no resistance, small, soft fingers that Trine can stroke inside.

•

A short while later: here we see Trine lifting Haldis up and holding her tight, feeling that she is finally home. Trine on the sofa: she lays Haldis down on her thighs while she pulls up her sweater, undoes her bra, and lifts Haldis to her breast. But unlike previously, Haldis doesn't throw herself forward, holding the breast with both hands; she's reticent, looks up at Trine, Trine nudges her nipple toward her mouth, and Haldis purses her lips and turns her head away, away from the breast. Oh, Haldis, Trine says. She tries again, nudges her breast toward her mouth, thrusts her shoulder forward to make it easier, and again, Haldis looks at her, sideways, takes the nipple tentatively, tries, but then lets go and turns her head even more, she arches her back and tries to get away. Trine can't understand. She packs up her breast again and walks around the living room with Haldis, looks at interesting things, points at the cars out on the street, looks at the print of Picasso's *La femme-fleur*, and sees that the female flower—Trine has never thought of it this way before—has two enormous breasts, perfectly round on each side of the stalk, perfectly round as though they were bursting with milk, and Trine points at the breasts and says, look! Boobies! But Haldis shows no enthusiasm for the boobies, instead she looks at a pigeon that has landed on the windowsill, and waves her arms around so the pigeon flies off again.

•

Here we see Trine, a little later, sitting with Haldis on her lap. Haldis is wriggling and crying, turning away from the breast, Trine has a tearful expression on her face, but *Haldis*, she says. Trine has to do the following: put Haldis down in an armchair, cut open a packet of formula, pour it into a bottle, and heat it in warm water. Haldis reaches out for the bottle impatiently, and says *mmm! mmm!* Maybe it's because I smell different, Trine thinks, maybe it would help if she'd taken a shower first and smelled of home, put on the clothes that are lying in the bedroom, change her bra and pads, maybe she smells of smoke.

•

Just before eight, it's time for the bedtime routine, and Trine almost feels nervous. She's showered, changed her clothes, and has to feed Haldis before she goes to sleep. Trine sits on the edge of the bed, Haldis lies on her thighs, and when she sees the breast approaching, she turns away and purses her lips. Haldis doesn't want it anymore. She's kind of *over* that stage.

•

And Trine hasn't had time to milk herself when she sits down at the table and gives Haldis a bottle, and as she looks down at the little mouth, sucking and sucking, she thinks to herself that she's experienced that for the last time, she's held Haldis to her breast for the last time, and Haldis has held her hands on either side of the breast as though she was scared it would suddenly go away for the last time, and Trine has heard the small sounds of her swallowing for the last time, no, she hasn't heard that for the last time, because she can hear them now, but it's different, because now it's not her milk she's drinking, though she's held Haldis in that particular way for the last time, into her skin, while stroking the wisps of hair on her head. For the last time, for the last time! Trine looks at the bottle, offended, and feels herself begin to cry, she's jealous of that bottle, she is, jealous of a bottle, how is that possible? Trine wonders harshly, but she knows that it's true, and she wants to scream, because she feels that something has been lost, something is gone, and she doesn't *want* it to be gone! Is this what it's like to be a mother? Is being a mother like everything else? Trine thinks, and starts to cry again, but carefully, she doesn't want to frighten Haldis, the crying is like that of a polar bear mommy, if polar bear mommies cried, and didn't just howl long, deep howls.

17

The Egyptian Collection is empty. The mummy room is empty. The rooms are full of Egyptian art and mummies, nothing else. And Linnea, who's walking around with a feeling in her chest that is both hopeful and stupid. Here she is, standing by the glass display cabinet, looking at the two mummies inside. And then suddenly she feels that there's someone standing in the doorway to the room, and she freezes in place.

·

But it's Robert, not Göran, who comes into the room, as if he didn't know that she was going to be here right now, and he says oh hello! so this is where you are.

·

(For your information, Göran is standing at the front of an auditorium with students sitting in all ten rows of seats, he's red in the face, and the sweat is running down his temples, he apologizes profusely, first he slept in, and then the car wouldn't start, so he had to cycle over on the icy roads, but never has a lecture on *Don Quixote* had a more appropriate start, he says, and the students laugh affably. So, Göran says, and leafs through his notes with shaking hands, today we're going to talk about *form*, about *Don Quixote* as a *novel*, and I thought I'd start by showing you a picture. He rummages for a transparency, puts it down on the overhead projector, looks back and discovers that he hasn't pulled down the screen, pulls it down and presses the on button on the projector. So, what have we here? Can anyone tell me? The students look at the screen, and what they see is a strange, knotted shape that looks like a stone, but with a hole in it, as though someone has cut right through. Could it be a fulgurite? is the suggestion from the auditorium. Göran looks up in surprise: ah, so someone out there is familiar with the mineral kingdom! he exclaims, and yes, it is a fulgurite. And why do I want to show this picture? Göran smiles: obviously I'm only doing it so I can get my breath back before I start the lecture. The students laugh. Well, Göran says, I do actually have another reason for it. We're going to talk about *Don Quixote* as a novel. A fulgurite is a formation that occurs when lightning strikes sand. The sand around the strike melts and turns to glass. Fulgurites come in all kinds of shapes, but they all have the same components: lightning and sand. Today, in short, I will claim that lightning is the *individual perspective* that strikes the sand of the literary epic and creates a new form: the novel. He pauses and holds up a book by Georg Lukács: first, Lukács, in short, Göran says. Lukács argues that the epic is a genre that is about, deals with, and works for and within an entire social group, whereas the novel is about the individual, and the problematic relationship between society and the individual. And *Don Quixote* is reckoned to be the very first novel—and here, indeed, we have an individual who is at odds with his surroundings, poor Don Quixote in his rickety coat of armor. And we mustn't forget that Lukács also argued that Dante's *Divine Comedy* was the last epic poem and the first novel: the novel being the genre of the fumbling human being. It's this fumbling . . . Göran looks up at the fulgurite and says nothing more, he looks at the fulgurite, and then he looks at the clock on the wall above the door, it's a quarter past ten, and then he looks at his hands, and then he looks at his keys that are spread out like a fan on the desk in front of him, and he suddenly remembers his dream, about the rattling bunch of keys that flashed in the glare from the overhead strip lighting, and he doesn't know why he dreamed it, what is it about the keys, and he looks at his students, who are waiting for him to carry on, who are waiting for the next words, "human being," but Göran has lost his thread, it's this fumbling . . . he starts again, *human being!* someone calls out. Thank you! Göran says, human being, yes, that's it.)

•

So this is it, Robert says, the mummy room. It's amazing, he says, and Linnea says yes, with a slightly disappointed smile. But it can't be disappointment—after all, he sat and read the brochure Linnea gave him and the more he read, the more certain he was that she'd had a reason for giving him the brochure, and the more certain he was that he was meant to interpret this, and that he was interpreting it correctly: it said in the brochure that art was a magic tool for the Egyptians. The paintings and hieroglyphics on the coffins were magic formulas, and they believed that what was portrayed would actually happen. What was portrayed *would actually happen*. These words made his palms sweat, is that what she means? Was that what she meant? That he should stand in the room, and that she would stand in the room, and that he was the one who would put his arm around her waist and kiss her, as she'd written in the screenplay she wanted "him" to do? Is it him she's wanted, all this time? Robert has completely forgotten that he has to tell her that the film won't be made. Linnea looks down at the display case and says: Did you know that the Egyptians separated the soul into five elements? Yes, he knew that, she'd written about it in the screenplay, it was "portrayed"! He doesn't say that, because then he'd ruin everything, his heart just pounds faster and faster, because why would she say that now, exactly the same words as in the screenplay? They separated it, Linnea says, as though reciting something by heart, into Ib, Sheut, Ren, Ba, Ka. The heart, the shadow, the name, the unique personality, and the life-force. And as she says this, she somehow knows: Göran won't be coming. This is never, for Linnea. This is what never feels like, Linnea thinks, and carries on, with a lump in her throat, and says that they often portrayed Ba, the unique personality, as a bird that flew out of the burial chamber, so it could find its way back to Ka, vitality, in the afterlife. It's actually rather beautiful, Linnea says, because then you can be reborn. One's unique personality can meet the general life-force and be reborn. That's so, so beautiful, she says in a whispering voice that suits her so well, like the small forest flower she's named after, and Robert thinks it's now, it's now he should put his arm around her waist, isn't it?

18

Here we see Dante. He's standing alone in the middle of an
endless plain, and it's snowing heavily all around him. He
starts to walk, but trips on something under the snow, a kind
of tussock. He kicks it and feels there's something stuck in it,
he starts to dig away the snow and a frozen blue face emerges;
it's Sigrid's face. And under Sigrid's head, which is stuck, not
to a body, but to the top of another tussock, he digs out
Linnea's face. And Trine's head and teary face are attached to
Linnea's neck on the one side, and on the other are Wanda's
head and teary face. He digs deeper, and under Linnea's head
he finds Elida's. Elida opens her eyes and when she sees that
it's Dante standing there, her eyes fill with tears, which immediately turn to ice. Dante is perplexed. He carries on dig-
ging and finds Viggo's head. It's frozen with a worried frown
between his eyebrows. And right at the bottom, he sees
Göran's white scalp, but his face is turned toward the earth.
Dante! someone shouts behind him, and he turns. It's Virgil,
who is struggling through the snow toward him, with a head

in each hand: it's Kåre and Robert. We're in the wrong place, Virgil puffs. This isn't where we're meant to be! he says, and throws the two heads down on the pile of other heads. Okay, Dante says, now I understand. I knew I'd never seen any of them before. And then he covers the heads again, almost carefully, with snow. So, he says to Virgil, and claps his mittens together to knock off some of the snow, shall we be off, then?

19

These buns are really good, Kåre says, and takes another bite. They're still soft and warm, and Kåre and Sigrid are still a bit puffy-faced after all the crying earlier in the day. They're sitting on the sofa, each in their part of Kåre's men's pajama set, Kåre wearing the bottoms and Sigrid the top, they've had sex again (there's no reason not to have sex, Kåre had thought, when you've already done it once), they're eating buns and Sigrid is exhausted to the very tips of her fingers. So what are we going to do about us? Sigrid says, because she thinks it was so nice when he said that in the café that time, and she said that they could kiss. He gives her a strange smile, but doesn't answer. Yes, what are we going to do, he says, staring into space. We could get married and have children, Sigrid says, because she has decided that she has to be genuine and direct and say things straight, but as she says it she hears that it's not quite as sassy as "well, we could kiss," especially since it was her who got him to repeat the question. There's a ring at the door. Kåre has a strange expression on his face.

Who could that be? he says, I don't know that I can be bothered to answer. Oh, Sigrid says, I forgot to say, it's probably someone called Ståle who came by earlier today when you were asleep, and I wrote down on a piece of paper that he would come back at five, but then we were so busy crying that I forgot to tell you, she says, but he doesn't laugh, hmm, says Kåre, who clearly doesn't want to open the door. He's forgotten that he, out of habit—an age-old habit to be fair, but all the same, now that he was free from everyone and everything after splitting up with Wanda, and was starting out on something new, and the thought of green, no, it was white, months just fizzed up in him, he'd come to the conclusion that having "a real blowout" (which we embarrassingly have to quote him on) might be fun—had rung up Ståle, his old contact, who doesn't live far from here. He'd completely forgotten. Are you scared it's Wanda? Sigrid asks, in a rather flat voice; no, I'm not, Kåre says, without knowing that Wanda is standing just down the street with a hammering heart because she's decided to go and ring his bell and ask if maybe they couldn't try again, she loves him, she really does, she doesn't think she can live without him, she's realized, and is now standing down the street with her hand on her forehead, she just has to pause a moment, her legs feel weak. What's holding you back, she's thought over and over this past week. A few principles, that's all.

•

What would have held her back, naturally, if she'd known about it, was the fact that Kåre was sitting there in his pajama bottoms and another woman was sitting beside him in his pajama top, and the other woman had just said that she

wanted to marry him and have his babies. But what would
have made her happier, Wanda that is, was if she'd known
that Kåre didn't react to what the other woman said in the
way that the other woman dearly hoped he would react, instead he reacted with a kind of claustrophobia. And if she
had known, Wanda, that the sharing pajamas thing was a
test on Kåre's part, though he was fully aware it was an idiotic test, but *all the same*: he wanted to see Sigrid in a pajama
top similar to the one that Wanda had appropriated as soon
as she moved in with him, without even thinking about it,
and left him freezing in his pajama bottoms, and he wanted
to see if he got the same feelings for Sigrid as he'd had for
Wanda when she wandered around the room with bare legs in
the oversized pajama top, and with her black hair that was
normally so straight and silky now attached to her head as
though it was unaware of itself, as though the ever hard and
cool Wanda had disappeared and the real, inner Wanda had
appeared in her place. And she would have been a bit happier, Wanda, if she'd known what Kåre had thought earlier
this morning when he woke up, before he got up and made
scrambled eggs: that he suddenly remembered what had happened during the night, that he had been woken suddenly by
something tickling his chin, and that, for a wonderful split
second, he'd thought that it was Wanda who was there, as
always, and in that split second understood that it wasn't
Wanda, but Sigrid, and that the familiar feeling of hair
against his chin was in fact an *unfamiliar* feeling, there was
an unfamiliar woman in his bed, who was now sitting on
his sofa and saying that she wanted to marry him and have his
babies. He didn't even really know her! And it would have

made her even happier, Wanda, if she had known that when Kåre was sitting there on the sofa and eating buns, feeling slightly awkward, because he wasn't a man who ate buns, he didn't particularly like biscuits and cakes, and certainly not buns—their only redeeming feature was that they were round and soft—if Wanda had known that Kåre, feeling slightly awkward about eating the buns baked by Sigrid, looked at Sigrid as she sat there watching television in his oversized pajama top, which she had buttoned up almost all the way, with hair that was much thicker and somehow more self-conscious than Wanda's thin black hair, and had suddenly and somehow known that it was over. Click: blackout.

20

Here we see George W. Bush. He's just woken up and looks around with obvious surprise in his eyes, he has no idea where he is because it's pitch-black all around his bed, the narrow bed with white bed linen stretches out far in front of him, maybe even sixty-five feet or so, like a breakwater narrows out into the sea; George W. Bush sits up in bed and turns his head, he lifts up his duvet and sees that he has a thin book wedged between his legs, he lifts it up and reads: *Golf Can't Be This Simple*, it says, and then he remembers, yes, he was reading this before he fell asleep, he's going to play golf with his father today, but now it looks like he might have ended up somewhere strange, he gets up and starts to walk down the bed-breakwater, and he looks so fragile all of a sudden as he walks along in his flannel pajamas, his body language wary, what in God's name is this, he thinks as he comes to the end of the breakwater: there's a ladder leading down from the edge of the bed, an iron ladder, straight down: well, I don't have a choice, do I, says Bush, and starts to climb down. Suddenly he sees glowing lava all around him, pouring down, like a stage curtain, everywhere, and he sees himself going down and down something that resembles a shaft: he looks down, he sees green grass down there and feels relief, because he was really starting to wonder, for a second or two, where on earth he was heading, but green grass is good, there's no green grass in hell, and the closer he gets, the greater the certainty that he knows where he is, and it's as though he is filled, slowly, with a kind of inner serenity, because the grass stretches out and out, he can see endless plains, I see the valley of peace below, Bush thinks, *of peace*, just that, *of peace*, it fills him with a kind of humility, as though he was full of warm tears, he puts his foot down on the grass and understands: he's at the heart of the world, the center of the earth, and he is filled with a peace he didn't know it was possible to feel, it just flows out of every atom in his body, it's almost as if I could float, Bush thinks, what if, he thinks and tries to lie back with his hands held out from his body, as in water, and it works: when he lifts his legs, he floats! What the heck, I'm floating, Bush shouts, and then he wakes up and sees that he's not at the center of the earth and he's certainly not floating, he's in his usual bed, in the big white house, and he probably hit his wife, his small white wife, in the face when he threw out his arms, but hasn't woken her, thankfully, she's lying asleep by his side. He wipes his brow, because that was the most incredible dream he's ever had. He looks over at the bedside table, at *Golf Can't Be This Simple*, which his wife gave him as a present, and touches it as though it were an object he'd never seen before, a dream object that will give him untold experiences.

21

Kåre sits in Kåre's living room and feels that he's done with crying, that he doesn't feel anything, the old cynicism that he'd been so upset about, it just came over him, and he felt no resistance, because the hair that was going to wake him up in the middle of the night had to be Wanda's. And if Wanda had known that, it would have been a lot easier to stand farther down the street with a hammering heart, hesitating. And now, Kåre thinks, he just needs to tell Sigrid, who's sitting here chewing, one cheek bulging with a slightly too big bite of bun. It just cascades out of him. Out.

•

In the future, this experience of having a woman he doesn't know in the house, and not least in his bed, and who then says she wants to marry him and have his babies even though she doesn't know him, will haunt him like a ghost, from the time when Kåre, in the middle of his life's way, found himself once again in a wood so dark that he couldn't tell where the straight path lay. Sigrid, who once upon a time for some peculiar reason appeared to be the light/salvation/Jesus, will eventually become a kind of nymph or hulder figure, or even a kind of hulder disguise, a see-through and shabby shell of a nymph, a kind of vampiric, snake-like nymph who appeared and wanted to take everything that he had, her empty skin will be blown away by the wind in his memory, but then get caught on a flagpole and hang there flapping, forever, and he will perhaps shudder when he picks up a whole frozen trout from the freezer in some supermarket, which he's going to take home and bake in the oven with mustard and dill, shudder as the memory of the hulder skin just pops up in his head as soon as his fingers touch the frozen tail, shudder at the thought that he almost swapped the ultimate woman for a hulder, for—and here Kåre stops with his hand on the trout tail—*the Green-Clad Woman*, he thinks, as though he's just realized, Ibsen's Green-Clad Woman. We chuckle when we hear this, because Sigrid was indeed clad in green when she first met Kåre as she stood at the railing with the desperate feeling that she was locked inside herself, that everything was locked inside, but that she recognized this, and that her recognition of this meant that the things she saw and experienced had therefore not lived, or existed, in vain. Sigrid, who is now sitting on Kåre's sofa, in his pajama top, which is buttoned all the way up, a living little girl with bare thighs and the uncomfortable feeling of not being able to deal with all this, not wanting to sit here, of perhaps having never felt so alien.

•

But now Kåre, where he's sitting on the sofa, feels nothing other than that it's over and that this is fine, and it almost makes him happy, in a way he's completely *over* the situation, in a physical sense, he knows what lies ahead and what lies behind, he knows that Sigrid is sitting here and is a girl whom he's going to hurt, but not yet, he also knows that he's a man who loves another woman and this, the fact that he *loves* another woman, overwhelms him, it's no longer there, the utter cynicism and cold, he loves, loves, and loves Wanda, and he jumps up from the sofa and says that he's going to find the picture of George Bush and George W. Bush, so she can see it, and Sigrid naturally misinterprets this, she notices that he's somehow lighter, even though he's more angular, sharper in a way, and she sighs with relief, things will get better now, she thinks, they're over the worst. And when he comes back with the photograph of the Bushes, she's glad, even though she thinks it's a shame that he's gotten dressed, that she's the only one still sitting there in pajamas and so is somehow more naked. But she looks at the photograph of the Bushes and thinks how strange it is, that now she's sitting on his sofa, in his pajamas, and looking at the photographs he talked about when they were in the café, she's kind of meeting herself again, but from a point further ahead in time, when everything has turned out okay, when her arms have stopped trembling with so much tension that she couldn't get the soup to her mouth, they've sorted things out, and she looks at George Bush Senior who has his arm around George Bush Junior, George Bush the son, who is wearing a life jacket and has reflective strips on his arms, he looks a bit helpless as he stands there with two fishing rods and Bush the father looks like he's a *father*, with all the strength it takes to embrace his son and help him, and she thinks that her interpretation of the picture now is that it's her, they're both her, the two versions of her, now she's the father who has the strength to embrace the previous version of herself, sitting there in the café, so uncertain and fumbling, she's embracing her now and can help her with everything. Even though, she thinks, she would rather be someone other than father and son Bush. Kåre thinks roughly the same thing when he sees the picture, he thinks that he's Bush Senior, with his arm around Bush Junior, and that they are both versions of himself. But in contrast to Sigrid's interpretation, this is an interpretation that leads him away from Sigrid, the strong Bush is the old Kåre and the young Bush is the Kåre he's become since he left Wanda in the belief that his cynicism had finally gotten the upper hand, that he could never love *her*, that even *she* irritated him and left him cold. Now he knows it wasn't like that. He loved her! Obviously, it wasn't just the pajama test, the unfamiliar hair against his chin during the night, and the sudden, overwhelming feeling of embarrassment at the freshly baked buns that made him recognize it, in a lightbulb moment—hadn't he already realized it back in the café when Sigrid started to talk about *Mrs. Dalloway*, out of the blue, as though literature was what was most important when you saw two planes crashing into the Twin Towers? And the fact that she was so uncertain, so fumbling; he'd tried to be fair, to be open-minded, tried to tell himself that this was a part of the new him, that he would accept her hesitations and wait until the essential and confident Sigrid appeared, but it seemed that Sigrid never would arrive, Kåre thought, and what he got out of all of this was only: Wanda. Wanda. What a wonderful name, Kåre thinks, and he lets

out a little laugh; what are you laughing at? Sigrid asks, nothing, Kåre says, and squeezes her shoulders. All they needed to
do now was get through the next few days, after which Sigrid
would be gone again. Sigrid jumps up. It's time to read the
poem she'd thought about reading to him before, to try to tell
him just how much it means to her that he sees her. I want to
read you a poem, Sigrid says, and Kåre says oh, and gives a
strained smile, yes. Hang on a moment, it's in my coat pocket.
Kåre already feels uncomfortable and hopes this will be over
soon. She's not exactly making it any easier for him. Sigrid
comes back with a small piece of paper that she's torn from
an envelope, or it looks like that, because he can see the plastic window where the address ought to be: I wrote it down
before catching the train, Sigrid says, because it says so much
about me, and who you are for me. Kåre says: okay, let's hear
it. Sigrid: *Drift.* (Oh no, she can feel that she's blushing!) My
life is adrift on the Arctic Ocean. (She blushes more and
more, because her voice sounds so clumsy, the words sound
so clumsy! *My life is adrift on the Arctic Ocean!* She realizes too
late that this isn't something to be read out loud to someone.
That only in silence and solitude can this strike you as the
deepest truth of your being. But she has to continue, now
that she's decided to read it, she has to stick to her decisions:)
My ship frozen in desolation. (Kåre looks embarrassed! She
has to say it:) I hear every crack and thud, does the current I
believed in sleep? (It's getting easier now, the blush is ebbing
and she reading with more force:) The wind sweeps over the
ice, but in the heavens the old markers shine bright. Yet
there is hope of breaking through. (She looks at him.) And
the dreams suck heavy clusters of stars. Sigrid gives a deep

bow. Kåre claps. Is the slightly old-fashioned language okay? Sigrid asks in a trembling voice. Her knees are trembling too, her hands try to smooth out the torn envelope without trembling. Yes, of course, Kåre says, I've read similar things before. What a fantastic poem, he says. I can recognize myself in it. He wants this situation over with fast! Sigrid smiles, feels her cheeks twitching, her heart beating nervously, I just wanted to say, Sigrid says, and looks down at her thighs, which are naked, and she feels the tears welling up in her eyes and then falling down onto her thighs. That you've led me safely through. Kåre: Oh, I'm glad, Sigrid. But he feels his insides *lurch*, he'd better tell her soon that he's *not* her way through! Or maybe it's best to wait until she's home again?

22

This is what Sigrid should have known when she sat in the café a month before and tried to get the soup to her mouth but couldn't because she was so nervous. But naturally, she didn't know, and that's the way it is, one doesn't know what's going to happen a month from now. So she just sits there in the café trying to get the soup to her mouth, and we so desperately want to help her, to hit her on the arm or something so she stops trembling, so she can eat her soup like any other normal person.

•

But that, strictly speaking, is not within our domain.

FINAL COMMENTS

Everything said here about George W. Bush is taken from the article "43+41=84" from Vanity Fair, *September 2006.*

Everything said here about George W. Bush's dream about the center of the earth is entirely made up.

Everything said here about the earth's crust is taken from forsk ning.no/evolusjon-paleontologi/2008/02/tidlig-liv-kan-ha-formet -jorda.

Everything said here about earthquakes is taken from www .jordskjelv.no/jordskjelv/om-jordskjelv/hva-er-et-jordskjelv/.

Everything said here about the Greenland shark's eating habits is taken from www.shark.ch/Database/Search/species.html?sh_id =1134.

Here you can find Golf Can't Be This Simple: *www.amazon .com/Golf-Cant-this-Simple-Swing/dp/097192080X.*

Most of what's said here about Paul de Man is fictional.

The parts that aren't fictional are based on a lecture by Arild Linneberg about Paul de Man's life, which we snuck into. So our thanks to him!

Sigrid's photograph of Paul de Man can be found in the book Responses: On Paul de Man's Wartime Journalism, *ed. Werner Hamacher, Neil Hertz, and Thomas Keenan (Lincoln: University of Nebraska Press, 1989). The photograph is by Ken Laffal Photography.*

Most of what's said here about Sofia Coppola is based on interviews and documentaries.

In addition, it should be said that there is some doubt about the word "the" that Linnea devotes so much energy to interpreting in Richard Brautigan's poem, which Göran left in her pocket before he went home to Lotta. Göran had just found those poems on the Internet (www.brautigan.net), and Göran copied the poem faithfully from there, and the website has several such words in brackets, and Göran didn't know whether the brackets were Brautigan's own or the website's, or what their function was. But he had to copy them.

It should also be added that Linnea interpreted the poem slightly differently than Göran intended; for Göran, the most important bit was the fact that the winds (in other words, he and Linnea) blew past. And that they were like dreams. And dreams are not real, as we know. Dreams, big and small, are passing, like the wind. Nor did Göran know that "te" is the Japanese word for hands. So it was not a holding *movement he had intended when he gave her the poem, quite the contrary, it was a* slipping away, passing *movement. In short: you and I, Linnea, are not made for each other. We are dreams that pop up and then vanish. We are winds that blow past.*

It happens!

Likewise, the words written on Karen Kilimnik's picture of the pale blue glitter horse, which we reported as stating that said horse was taking someone to the glitter palace, aren't entirely correct.

What it actually says, in fact, is "My Pony Arriving to Pick Me Up at the Glitter Theater, St. Petersburg 2000."

Any similarities between the fictional characters herein are completely accidental.

Likewise the fact that they quote the same literary works.

The poem that Sigrid quotes on page 72 is from Olav H. Hauge's collection Dropar i austavind *(Samlaget, 1966).*

•

The poem that Sigrid should have quoted, perhaps, is this one by Ivar Aasen:

I know so well there is a heart
That feels the same as mine,
That yearns the same and hurts the same,
And shares my hope, my time.

And if I found it, all would be well
And life would flow untroubled.
But this is painful to recall:
We never found each other.

But things do eventually go well for Sigrid; we can disclose that here in these final comments. In fact, things are already much better by June, her eternal suffering has eased little by little after all, and so she finally dares go up to the railing again. She walks up and feels—partly because it's warmer and she's wearing a T-shirt, of course—as though the yoke of winter is falling from her shoulders, and when, at the signal of a gust of wind, small, flat seeds start to shower down from the trees on the long avenue that leads up to the railing, she's overwhelmed by the sight and has to stop: as though great snowflakes of transparent bronze are sparkling around her. She has to stretch out her arms (that is to say, she of course doesn't stretch them out, someone might see her, after all, standing there like an idiot with her arms outstretched, but she feels that she has to stretch out her arms) in the shower of glittering bronze seeds because she feels everything is quivering: something is about to happen, something is on its way, that's how she would prefer to put it, and even though she doesn't know what it is, and even though it might very probably be something very small, it's something that is, at least, possible.

•

Phew, and let that be our final comment.

•

*With love from Beatrice and Dulcinea
(who have, of course,* been your narrators and guides)*

---

*"Of course" because we are the perfect narrators for this story; see *The Divine Comedy* by Dante and *Don Quixote* by Cervantes. As Sigmund Skard says: "Dante saw Beatrice for the first time when he was nine, and she was a little younger. She was wearing a deep red dress. And in that moment 'the vital spirit, that which dwells in the most secret chamber of the heart, began to tremble so violently that I felt it fiercely in the least pulsation.' Whenever he then sees her again, he proclaims that she is so noble that she cannot be of this earth: she must be 'the daughter of a God.' Many years were then to pass—a further nine. Dante then meets Beatrice in the street and the meeting feels like a wedding. She is now dressed in white, and she greets him with a smile that sends him straight to heaven. The following night, in his intoxication, he sees Love itself: it holds Beatrice in its lap and Dante's burning heart in its hand. She is given his heart to eat and is then transported to heaven in tears. Beatrice thus becomes more of a symbol than a person to him, a symbol of what we now call sublimation." No woman embodies more clearly the image that Sigrid struggles with at the start of this novel, that of the sublime woman in an oversized shirt, than Beatrice! say I, Dulcinea—even though eating a heart is rather earthy and physical. You're right about that, say I, Beatrice, but there is a woman who has been sublimated to an even greater degree, and that is Dulcinea del Toboso. I, Dulcinea, blush, okay,

okay, say I, Dulcinea, and hide my face in my small red hands. The fact is, say I, Beatrice, that Dulcinea is a very ordinary and not particularly beautiful country girl, on the contrary, she is rather coarse, unsophisticated, and unattractive, but in Don Quixote's vivid imagination she is transformed, or sublimated, if you like, into a beautiful and desirable virgin whom he worships with all his beating heart. In more or less exactly the same way that Kåre transformed Sigrid into a kind of Jesus, whereas she was actually a kind of vampire. I, Dulcinea, smile and shake my head. But naturally, you are not coarse and unsophisticated, Dulcinea, say I, Beatrice, and give her a hug. Thank you, say I, Dulcinea. And now we bid you farewell!

(Both break into song, a very brief excerpt of the beautiful "Mrs. Bartolozzi" by Kate Bush, in which the song's "I" thinks she sees "you" standing outside, but it's only a shirt):

Hanging on the washing line
Waving its arms as the wind blows by
And it looks so alive

(Both wave as they get smaller and smaller in the distance.)